01

Praise for Lauren Dane's *Making Chase*

2007 CAPA winner Best Contemporary Romance

4 ½ Stars "Dane takes the age-old tale of love between a high-society guy and a girl from the wrong side of the tracks and makes it new again in this delightful page-turner."

~ *Romantic Times*

Recommended Read "I laughed, I cried, and boy did I gasp. The emotions were just out of control throughout this book, in a good way of course. For Ms. Dane to be able to pull all of those reactions from a reader is a testimonial to her fantastic writing skills"

~ *FAR*

Recommended Read "Lauren Dane packs Making Chase with very hot love scenes that demonstrate the emotions these two feel for one another. I have to say, I will miss this family and am sorry to see the series end. I know that I will be rereading these books often and, as Making Chase is by far my favorite, I will most likely wear out my copy!"

~ *Two Lips Reviews*

Recommended Read "If the first three books in this series haven't been read, I recommend wholeheartedly reading each and every one. While Making Chase by Lauren Dane can stand alone, the full effect of this wonderful family is a must read experience. I joyfully recommend it!"

~ *Joyfully Reviewed*

Five Blue Ribbons "I've loved every book in this series and they've all pulled at my emotions in one way or another. Ms. Dane saved the one brother we were all dying to know about for the last story."

~ *Romance Junkies*

"Author Lauren Dane weaves an enticing and romantic tale with MAKING CHASE. A blending of two families, a forever kind of love between our hero and heroine, and love scenes that sizzle, make this one book that should not be missed."

~ *Romance Reviews Today*

Look for these titles by *Lauren Dane*

Now Available:

Reading Between The Lines
To Do List

Chase Brothers Series:
Giving Chase (Book 1)
Taking Chase (Book 2)
Chased (Book 3)

Cascadia Wolves Series:
Wolf Unbound
Standoff
Unexpected

Making Chase

Lauren Dane

A Samhain Publishing, Ltd. publication.

Samhain Publishing, Ltd.
577 Mulberry Street, Suite 1520
Macon, GA 31201
www.samhainpublishing.com

Making Chase
Copyright © 2008 by Lauren Dane
Print ISBN: 978-1-59998-759-0
Digital ISBN: 1-59998-505-5

Editing by Angela James
Cover by Scott Carpenter

First Samhain Publishing, Ltd. electronic publication: June 2007
First Samhain Publishing, Ltd. print publication: June 2008

Dedication

I'm going to miss Petal. I've had so much fun writing these stories of this wonderful town and family. I want to thank Angie, who read and saw the potential in Giving Chase and for giving me a home with Samhain. I'm proud to say you're my editor and someone I count as a friend as well.

Ray, thank you for believing in me.

My fabulous friends Sparkles and Piston. Crit partners, shoulders, cheerleaders and all around fabulous goddess–type creatures. You two rock.

Beta chickies—I'm fortunate in the wonderful women who give me their time and read my books. Every single book I write is better because of their advice and suggestions. Special thanks goes to Tracy - thank you so much for being there even before I had a book published, your continual friendship and support means the world to me.

And truly, I cannot possibly thank my readers enough. Thank you to those of you who come to my chats, who hang out at my messageboard, who take the time from your busy lives to write me notes that keep me going! I am humbled by your support and love, you're all the best.

Chapter One

Tate Murphy sat in the comfy chair at her station, sipping coffee and looking out the window. It was a Saturday in the very beginning of February. Winter had been cold but spring was beginning to imagine itself. The trees carried buds, heavy with leaves and the air wasn't quite as chilly as it'd been even a week before.

All in all, a lovely day. Soon to be even lovelier. One leg crossed over the other, foot slowly kicking back and forth, she waited for her morning visual donut. Matt Chase.

Ah, there he was. *Hot damn,* her body lit up when he pulled his truck into the lot adjacent to the salon. Hopping out, he hefted a duffel bag over one shoulder and loped across the street.

"Good Lord the man looks good enough to eat," Tate murmured as she took a drink of her coffee. Faded jeans showed off long legs and a nice, trim booty. A hoodie sweatshirt fended off the cold but didn't stop her from seeing the work-hard body beneath. He was in dire need of a haircut and she had no trouble admitting she'd love to get her fingers in it. A bit shaggy, it curled up just around his ears and touched the back of his collar. A color like burnt sugar.

Although he had on cool-looking sunglasses, she knew the eyes beneath were a light green, fringed with chocolate lashes. Mmm. Mmmm. Mmmm.

"Ah, I see his hotness has arrived." Anne, co-owner and her next youngest sister, stood next to her, leaning into the chair.

"Kinda makes me want to set a fire," Tate said, one corner of her mouth lifting.

"Um, I smell something burning already. Your panties perhaps?"

Blushing furiously, she spun, laughing at Anne's outrageous comment. "I'm gonna light a candle for you. Three."

Anne joined her in laughter. "You just about raised me, I expect I need all the help I can get."

"Hey, divas, did I miss him?" Beth, the last owner and next youngest sister after Anne approached to refill everyone's coffee cup.

"Yeah, he just went inside. But there's always lunchtime." Sated for the morning, Tate stood and began to get all her tools in order, making sure her station was stocked and ready for the day.

Four years before, Tate and Anne had decided to buy the rundown old house at the far end of Main Street and renovate it into a hair salon. They'd scrimped, saved, worked multiple jobs and got the down-payment together and then had spent months doing the renovation work themselves. Luckily, they had a large, and free, workforce. With eight Murphy kids and two spouses to help, they'd been able to paint, knock out walls, drywall, replace the plumbing, landscape, and apply for all the proper permits and licenses. Hell, they'd even put up a new roof. A few months after Anne graduated from beauty school, Tate left her old salon in Riverton and they opened the doors to Murphy's Cuts and Curls.

Two years after that, Beth came in as part owner and ran the business end of things. The salon was a family affair. Beth had been helping out with the books when she'd offered to buy in at a smaller share. The place would wither and die without her to, well, do everything that needed doing. Not only did she handle the books and deal with ordering supplies but if someone needed a shampoo she could do that too.

Truthfully, Tate had wanted a fancier name but their youngest sister, Jill, who was getting her degree in marketing, told them that if they kept the name folksy but not too cutesy, it'd make people more comfortable.

Jill must have had something, because from the moment they'd opened, they'd done a brisk business. Women stopped leaving town to get their hair done. Tate and Anne offered everything from the giant hairspray helmet the women like Polly Chase preferred to the stylish razor cuts her daughter-in-law Liv currently sported. It made Petal seem a friendlier place to Tate, who always had felt an outsider there.

Tate made a decent living. Enough that she'd been able to help Tim and her other siblings pay tuition at the University of Georgia for their two youngest siblings. Before that, she worked to pay for her younger brother Nathan's college and master's in teaching. They'd all worked together to help out when the others had needed it and that's what counted.

"Anne, your first client of the day is a color, I'll send her over to Tate for the cut," Beth announced as she made another pot of coffee.

Tate looked at the place she and her sisters had built from the ground up and pride swelled her heart.

૮૭

Matt tossed his clothes into the hamper with his name on it and headed toward the showers. He'd been up for sixteen hours and was dead on his feet. Too bad he didn't have the luxury of sleeping, one of the other guys at the station had been injured at the fire they'd just put out and Matt needed to fill in for him.

As he quickly cleaned up, the scent of freshly brewing coffee cut through the steam, waking his senses. When he stumbled out into the main living area on the second floor of the firehouse, he saw his older brother Shane waiting for him.

"I heard about Tony getting hurt." Shane's voice was gruff as he handed Matt a cup of coffee. Matt knew it was Shane's way of making sure he was unhurt.

"He'll be all right. Jim had some smoke inhalation so he's at the hospital too, just to get checked out. I wasn't in the part of the house where the beams collapsed so I'm lucky."

"Here, Momma sent this over. She wanted to come herself, you know how she is. But Daddy intercepted her and I promised to bring it." Shane quickly covered his grin with a pathetic attempt at hunger as he handed a series of sealed containers to Matt.

"Come on, get that hangdog look off your face. I'm sure there's enough for five of us." Matt put the containers on the table and pulled out plates and utensils as Shane popped the lids off and made sounds of approval.

"Smothered pork chops, mashed potatoes, dang, she even sent over cornbread. Cassie's gonna kill me for spoiling dinner but I can't resist."

Matt snorted as he filled his plate. "Yeah, 'cause Cassie's such a fine cook and all."

Shane couldn't stifle a laugh but shook his head. "You're a bad influence on me. She may not be able to cook worth a damn but she makes up for it in other areas. Speaking of hot

12

sexy women, how're things going with Melanie?"

Matt shrugged. "Eh. She's..." he paused before sighing, "...vacant. Yeah, she's pretty and has a great body. She's good in bed and all, but she doesn't make me laugh. We don't *talk* about anything real. She doesn't seem to care about anything. Honestly, I want to have what you guys have. But the right woman hasn't come along yet."

"I used to think being married was being tied down and trapped. But Cassie, being with her changed me, changed my life. Even after being married a year and knowing her two, I haven't found myself bored yet. The woman is a roller coaster." Shane chuckled.

"Well, I'm a lucky man. My sisters-in-law are all firecrackers. I want that too. I'm wondering if I'll find her. I'm thirty-two, I've dated a lot of women within a thirty mile radius of Petal. Maybe she's not out there. Maybe I fucked up with Liv and I'll never get another chance."

"You didn't want Liv. You still don't. She's meant for Marc. All I can say is your woman is out there. I know it for a fact. I think you're looking in the wrong places. If you want a deep woman you can laugh with, stop going out with women like Melanie. Break the pattern, Matt."

Matt sighed as he ate. "Women like Melanie are familiar territory, you know?"

"I do know. I was you, Matt. Okay, better looking, but still, look at the women I kept ending up with. Except for Maggie, and we all know that was doomed. It wasn't until I clapped eyes on Cassie that I *knew* what I wanted. Her. Forever. It took Kyle a few months and Marc a few years of knowing their women. You? I think you're more like me. You'll see her and you'll know and it'll be right."

"You know, everyone in this town thinks you're such a

hardass. If they only knew what a sensitive person you were deep inside. I'm not being snide, I mean it. Thanks. Thanks for checking in on me and for the food and for caring."

"You're my brother, Matt. And my best friend. Although if you told Kyle or Marc, I'd have to say I love you all equally and crap because I'm the oldest and all."

Matt snorted and popped his brother one on the arm.

Chapter Two

"What brings you into my bookstore today, young man?" Cassie moved from behind the counter to kiss Matt's cheek and give him a hug.

"I just had lunch at The Sands and was on my way back to work so I thought I'd stop in to say hey." He turned at the sound of his name as his other sister-in-law came in. "I'm surrounded by Chase women. How are you feeling, darlin'?"

Liv accepted his kiss and gave one to Cassie, who rubbed Liv's stomach.

"I'm fine. That damned brother of yours and his super sperm. Who'da thought he'd have knocked me up so fast." Liv patted the barely perceptible swell of her belly.

"You said you wanted a husband and a family. Well, there you go. No April Fool's for your ovaries." Cassie winked.

"And all within four months. Marc moves fast." Matt was thrilled for his brother and Liv. Another grandchild for his parents and another niece or nephew to join Nicholas.

"Yeah, like honeymoon fast. Cassie got a tan on her honeymoon, I got a fetus!"

Suddenly, the screech of tires and screams sounded from outside. Matt turned and saw a car accident through the windows of the store. "Call 911!" he yelled as he headed toward the door.

He saw a woman lying in the street and his heart sped as his professional side took over.

"Everyone needs to back up. An ambulance is on the way." He knelt next to the woman, who groaned and put her hand up to her face. A trickle of blood oozed from a cut on her forehead. "Miss, how are you feeling?"

Her eyes fluttered open, bright blue eyes, and widened for a moment before she tried to sit up.

"No, stay still. I don't want you to move until I know more." Quickly and efficiently, he skimmed his hands over her. She'd received some abrasions on the backs of her arms where the pavement had ripped her shirtsleeves.

"I'm all right. Really. He wasn't even going that fast."

"What happened?" Shane jogged up as the ambulance arrived.

An elderly woman who'd apparently seen the accident came forward to explain as Matt and Shane helped the paramedics. "Charlie pulled away from the curb and Tate here got jostled. Bunch of boys from the high school on skateboards. Rushing to get back to school I'd wager. Anyway, looked to me like they rushed past and she got pushed out into traffic. He couldn't have been going too fast."

"Those boys need to be put in jail!" one of the gathered people called out.

"No, no, they didn't mean to hurt me. Honestly. They're just silly kids doing silly kid stuff. I'm just a bit scuffed up," the woman, the witness had called her Tate, said from the gurney.

"Miss Murphy, I'll send someone to the hospital to take your statement. Just get yourself over there and get checked.

Don't worry about anything else just now," Shane reassured her and Matt closed the doors to the ambulance and stepped back.

"I've got to get back to the station. I'll talk to you later. I didn't see anything but if you need a statement, you know where I'm at."

ଚ

No freaking way did Matt Chase rub up all over her while she lay sprawled in the street like a drunken hobo! Tate couldn't believe her luck. The closest she'd ever been to the man and of course she had to have a torn shirt, bleeding face and her back-of-the-drawer panties. *Special.* Well okay, so he didn't see her panties or anything but *she'd* known they were on. And she'd noticed, as Tim had insisted on driving her home, she'd spilled something or other on her shirt.

"Tate, honey, I doubt he noticed the stain on your shirt." Anne laughed as Tate regaled her with the story the following day.

"Well I suppose I should be glad I didn't toot or have a giant booger or something."

Anne snorted. "I can't believe you got hit by a car. What's the world coming to when teenaged boys shove a woman into the path of an oncoming car?"

"Drama much? They didn't shove me into the street and Charlie Wilks was doing five miles an hour tops. Which is only two miles an hour slower than he drives at full speed. He's a hundred-and-fifty years old, I'm just glad he stopped instead of thinking I was a blonde-headed speed bump."

"I still think you should have pressed charges."

"Their parents made them come to my house and apologize.

17

Really, Anne, they were sorry. And Tim scowled at them extra hard. You know that face."

"One of the only helpful things any of us got from Dad," Anne mumbled.

"I don't suppose either one of them bothered to call," Jill called out from her perch in the window seat, looking up from a book.

"Good Lord, go back to school already." Beth bustled past and put towels at everyone's stations. "You know they didn't and thank God for that. Mom is off with some dude in Dallas and Dad is in the bottom of a bottle. I doubt they even know Tate moved out much less got hit by a car."

"Children, please." Tate sighed as she shook her head. Jacob and Jill had come back to town immediately when they'd heard about the accident. Jacob was out working with Tim for the day at his plumbing business and Jill was doing some studying.

"Ahh, my ten o'clock is here." Anne turned and smiled as Polly Chase came click-clacking into the shop. "Good morning, Mrs. Chase! How are you today?"

Polly patted her hair and smiled. "I'm good, sugar. I've got a bit of a dent here in the back so I need a good, solid re-do from you. My roots may be in need of a bit of TLC too." She winked and Tate grinned. If there was a person who could resist Polly Chase, Tate hadn't met them yet.

"Good morning, Tate, honey. I hear you had a little run-in with Charlie's front bumper yesterday. You all right?" Polly's cheeky mood softened into concern. Tate was nearly as short as Polly so it wasn't hard to let herself get pulled into a hug.

"Oh I'm fine. Just a bump on the head. Both your sons were there to help though."

Polly brightened. Tate did love that about Mrs. Chase—the

way she doted on her family. What she wouldn't have given to have a mother like her instead of what they all got in Tina.

"Shane's the one who told me, but I haven't seen any of my other boys."

"Matt helped until the ambulance got there. He was very gentle." And he smelled really good.

"He's a good boy. They all are. I'm glad you're all right, honey. I would have called you right away last night but Maggie said she talked with Nathan and all your siblings were on the job. If you need anything at all don't you hesitate to ask." Of course, Nathan, Tate's brother the teacher worked with Maggie and would have told her all about it. Small town gossip moved fast.

"Thank you, Mrs. Chase. I appreciate that."

Anne helped Polly to the shampoo station. Draping her to protect her clothes, she got to work while Beth went to mix the color they'd need.

Tate had several cuts right in a row and kept busy for the rest of the day, in between her siblings dropping by the shop to check in on her.

At two-thirty she swapped out her teal-blue kitten heel slides for a pair of sneakers. "I'm going to pick Belle, Sally and Danny up from school. I'll be back in a few."

"Let me do it," Jill piped up.

"Look here, missy, you have an exam you need to study for. You shouldn't even be here. I can walk the four blocks to the grade school and pick them up and take them to William and Cindy's. Same as I do every Wednesday."

"You will not." Anne came into the reception area. "William is picking the kids up. I told you that this morning. Tate, you got hit by a car. A. Car. You can cut yourself a one day break."

"I made a commitment. They expect Aunt Tate to pick them up every Wednesday. Just as Uncle Nathan picks them up on Tuesdays and Auntie Beth on Fridays and mommies and daddies on other days. That's what family does. We keep our promises and we don't let each other down."

Anne pulled Tate into a hug and said softly into her ear, "You're not drunk or passed out in some hotel room with a stranger and they're not starving. Tate, honey, your family never doubts for a millisecond your commitment to them. We know. Belle, Sally, Danny and Shaye know you love them but got hurt yesterday. Let us help *you* for a change."

As she'd done many times in her life, she let her family make her feel better.

By the end of the day she was glad she'd listened because her muscles ached and her head hurt. The doctor had said she'd most likely have some soreness and a headache for a while on and off. She took some pain reliever and hoped for a quiet night for a change.

Jill drove her back home and Tate spent the last bit of nagging time to convince her sister and brother to get back to Atlanta and to school.

"After dinner, though." Jill grinned.

Tate was good at three things—cutting hair, dancing and cooking. She was so good at it her siblings, even as adults, could be found at her dinner table any given day of the week. She took great pride in these things. It was a good thing to have skills that made you happy and people could always use a meal, a bit of dancing and a trim. It wasn't rocket science but it made Tate special.

The driveway already had two cars in it and Tate smiled,

the tiredness ebbing as she found comfort in those people she loved most. Except for Tim, her siblings were almost like her children and rather than feeling burdened by it, it buoyed her, anchored and strengthened her.

Her house, a neat little bungalow in that area of town that hovered between decent neighborhood and neighborhood in decline, was her proudest possession, even more than the shop. It wasn't much. Just two bedrooms, a small living and dining room, but the kitchen was big and the bathroom was too.

She'd decided on a pretty butter yellow with light blue trim on the shutters. She was no green thumb though so William, a baker and gardener extraordinaire, took pity and did all the planting and managing of her yard.

It was her oasis from the world and was quite frequently teeming with Murphys. Luckily, while the house was small, the lot it sat on was gargantuan. She had a big, fenced-in backyard so her nieces and nephew could come over and play any time they wanted. Which was often enough she had a toy box in her living room and a play set out back.

"Looks like you're not the only one who wants to eat at my table tonight."

Jill laughed as she pulled Tate's car into her spot closest to the house. "Duh. You feeling okay? We can get take-out too. It's really just that I'd like to spend some more time with you before we go back tonight."

"I'm good. I just had a headache but it's going away now. I expect some food will help."

The scent of freshly baked bread greeted her when she walked inside. Nathan smiled from the kitchen. "Hey, sweetie. William brought several loaves of bread by. He said he'd see you tomorrow and to call if you need anything. I told him Jill and Jake are going back tonight and I'm sleeping over here so he didn't have to worry."

Nathan looked like he'd be the most laid back of the whole Murphy crew but in reality, aside from Tate, he was the most tenacious. She knew he'd sleep on her porch if she didn't give him the guest room so she didn't bother arguing.

"Thank you, Nate. I don't need it. I'm fine, of course, but as no one is listening to me, I'll save my breath. And yes, Jill and Jake are going back after dinner."

Beth wandered in and absently pressed a hand to Tate's forehead. "You're warm and you look tired. Why don't we get take out?"

"Yes. I'm calling right now. China Gate I think." Jill pulled out a menu and began to consult with Nathan. Tate just shook her head.

"Fine. Get extra egg rolls. I *am* going to bake some cookies though. Chocolate chip with walnut and oatmeal peanut butter chip I think."

"Dang, I think so too." Jacob walked into the living room, hair still wet from the shower. "Don't worry, the car is packed. I know you're kicking us out after we eat. But I wouldn't look amiss at some cookies to take home." He sent her puppy dog eyes.

She changed clothes and got started on the cookies. It didn't take long, she tended to have a basic mix in her fridge or freezer to add extras to because she baked so often.

Her siblings cleared the dining room table and laid out plates as she changed out baking sheets and cooled the cookies.

"Wow, you're sending that many home with us? You rock."

Tate rolled her eyes at Jacob. "No. You can have a third. Nate can take another third to his class, you said they had some kind of math-olympics thing, right? And the last third is a thank-you for the firefighter who helped me yesterday after the accident."

They ate a big dinner and saw Jill and Jacob off clutching enough food for the next few days. Beth left for her apartment a few blocks away and Nathan bunked down in her guestroom.

Tate sat in bed and stared at the television for a while, letting the cherished silence settle in around her. She had a very full and satisfying professional and personal life with her family. And yet, something was missing. She saw Anne with her boyfriend, Tim with Susan and William with Cindy and she wanted that too. She wanted a man to come home to. She wanted children of her own.

Would she ever have that? Would a fluffy girl like her be able to find a man who'd want the whole package? So okay, Tate knew she was a big girl and most days she was okay with that. She didn't really have problems being fat. She didn't even have issues with the word fat unless her father was the one using it. Using it to slap her, to punish her for not breaking, for helping the others survive.

But it wasn't just the abundant curves, it was the seven siblings, two sisters-in-law and their children.

It wasn't like her family was meddlesome so much as they were all very involved in each others' lives. Tate didn't have many friends she wasn't related to. Some men she'd dated had a problem with that. They'd felt like they didn't fit in or that she didn't drop everything for them. When she thought about the man she wanted to share her life with, she knew she wanted to share her family with him too. Wanted him to think those things were as important as she did.

She yawned so wide her jaw popped but at least it shook her out of her thoughts. Gawd, clearly the accident was making her maudlin. Time to go to sleep.

Chapter Three

Matt opened up the box and the heady scent of cookies greeted his senses. Mouth watering, he read the note, ascertained the cookies were from Tate, the woman he'd helped out earlier in the week after the car accident. He vaguely remembered her from school. Perhaps a year or so behind him, definitely not from his circle though.

Knowing she wasn't a terrorist, he gave in and shoved a chocolate chip cookie in his mouth. And moaned. Holy shit, that was the best thing he'd ever eaten, even better than Maggie or his momma's cookies though he'd never admit it to them. An oatmeal cookie followed. Nope, *that* was the best cookie he'd ever eaten. Peanut butter chips in oatmeal cookies? Fabulous. Thank goodness she'd been okay after she'd gotten whacked by that car. The world couldn't live without this cookie-baking goddess.

Looking at the outside of the box, he realized the address was the beauty salon just across the way. He'd have to go and thank her in person.

He'd saved some folks, helped at quite a few accidents and emergencies and fought fires in and around Petal for the last decade. Still, he could count the number of times he'd received a thank you note on one hand. It felt good to be appreciated.

Finishing up in the late afternoon, Matt grabbed what was left of the cookies, knowing he'd have to work out extra after the dozen or so he'd scarfed down since the mail came. He'd had to hide them from the rest of the weenies at the station who'd have swiped them if they'd known. And with cookies as good as the last five in the box, he wasn't gonna share.

He'd never been inside the beauty salon though he'd seen it just about every day for years. He had a vague idea that the women in his life got their hair done there, but that was the extent of it.

When he opened the door, the jingle of pretty wind chimes greeted him first, followed by the pleasing sound of feminine laughter. Oh how he loved the sound of a woman's laugh.

Smiling, he headed toward it. He saw her before she saw him. Her hair was the prettiest blonde he'd seen on a woman and unless he was mistaken, she came by it naturally. It hung in a high ponytail and still cascaded down her back in a long spiral curl. Those wide blue eyes of hers were set off by some floaty-looking blouse that was a sort of pinkish-orange. He was sure they had a name for it, women always had names for colors like that. He'd say that Nicholas had light green walls in his room but Maggie had told him they were sea foam green. He'd just looked at his brother over her head and Kyle rolled his eyes back at him.

She was short. Like really short. And all curves. Her musical laughter cut off when she caught sight of him and then began to choke.

Dropping his things on a nearby counter he rushed to her, concerned as she waved him off, her eyes widening as she backed away.

"She's all right," one of the other women said.

Tate recovered and turned a shade of red he was sure they

had a name for too, but it was clear she'd either injured herself or was mortified.

"Fuckety fuck," she muttered as she tried to catch her breath.

"Are you all right?" He touched her arm.

Her blush deepened as she nodded, sending her ponytail swaying. "Fine. Um, can't breathe and swallow at the same time. Apparently I forgot that."

He grinned. "I'm Matt Chase. I just wanted to come by to thank you for the cookies."

"Oh...oh, I'm glad you got them. I should have just brought them over but I didn't know when I'd get the chance to get away and my family was sort of trying to steal them and if I hadn't wrapped them up they'd have ended up at the University of Georgia with my kid brother and sister."

He couldn't stop grinning. The woman was like one of those little dogs with all the energy. "It's fine. They're really good. Like criminally good. In fact, and if you repeat this, I'll deny it, they're the best cookies I've ever eaten. You missed your calling you know. You should have opened a bakery."

"Her cookies are a drop in the bucket. She makes a peach cobbler that'll bring tears to your eyes and the most perfect scratch biscuit you ever tasted. That's until you try her chicken paprika," one of the women, clearly a relative, told him proudly.

"Stop it now. I already said you could have Saturday off." Tate winked and the other woman laughed. "Oh, my manners! I'm Tate Murphy. Aside from bleeding all over you the other day, I figure we haven't been formally introduced."

He shook her hand, still wearing a stupid grin.

"This is my sister, Anne and the sister just younger than her, Beth."

He nodded to all of them and noted they all had the same nose but they were redheads with green eyes while Tate had blue eyes and blonde hair. She was also a lot shorter than the other sisters, who were at least five-seven or so.

"Nice to meet you all. I think I know your brother Tim. He and I were just a year apart in school. We had a few classes together. Redhead right? Green eyes? Freckles?"

"That's our brother." Tate grinned.

"He's a nice guy. Tell him I said hello. Well, I don't want to keep you all. I just wanted to thank you for the cookies."

"Well, thank *you* for helping me. A few cookies are nothing in comparison."

He liked her smile. Wide, open.

"I'll see you around then." And he realized that he'd never bumped into her at all around town. Which was sort of silly considering they worked right across the street from each other.

"Night, Matt. Nice to meet you. Your mother talks about you all the time."

He stopped as he'd reached the door and heard her laugh. "You knew that'd get me, didn't you?" he said, looking back over his shoulder at her.

Her eyes widened in mock surprise. "Me? I have seen you naked though. With a cowboy hat on even."

He groaned, knowing the picture. His momma did love to show that picture of him at about eighteen months old, naked as a jaybird wearing a cowboy hat.

"Are you imagining me naked now?" he teased back and she blushed bright red again. He toyed with asking her what women would call that shade of red but decided against it. He winked and waved. "See you around, Tate Murphy."

He whistled all the way to his truck.

"Fuckadoodledoo. I cannot believe I nearly choked to death on my own spit when I caught sight of the man in my own shop." Tate fell into a chair and put her face in her hands.

Beth chuckled. "He's so handsome I'm surprised you could talk. Nice too. And clearly, he liked you, Tate."

"Oh yeah, 'cause I'm totally his type." Tate rolled her eyes.

"Stop it," Anne said harshly.

"What? Come on, Anne. You've seen the women on his arm. What do they have in common with me other than like, having skin and hair and basics like that? You know what the Chase wives look like."

"I won't hear you speak about yourself in his voice, Tate. I won't, damn it. You are the best woman I know. Period." Anne was so vehement it took Tate back a bit.

Tate stood and hugged her sister. "Hey, I'm not putting myself down. I swear to you. But I'm being realistic. Anne, there's a place between Dad and being totally delusional. Matt Chase dates tall, strikingly beautiful, *thin* women. I am none of those things. Oh, now let me finish! I'm attractive in my own way but I'm five foot one and not thin and while I wouldn't crack mirrors, I am not strikingly beautiful like Jill or Beth."

Beth snorted. "You're the best of us, Tate. I don't know a woman more beautiful than you are and that's the honest truth. I do have very nice knockers though not as big as yours."

They laughed, the tension broken by Beth's silly comment.

"We on for Martini Friday?" Anne kissed Tate's cheek and squeezed Beth's arm.

"Hell yeah. My place in two hours. No boys allowed. I picked up vodka yesterday and I've been marinating the chicken

29

and shrimp all day." Tate grinned.

Tate went home and tried not to think about what an utter lameass she'd been in front of Matt Chase. Choking, blushing, making that stupid crack about him being naked and then his question. If she'd known him better she'd have told him the truth. Hell yes she'd been imagining him naked. Had done for years now. It was her daily pastime. She got bored? Picture Matt Chase nekkid and at her beck and call. Waiting for the dentist? Imagine Matt Chase having her be naked and at his beck and call. Oh so many variations on such a fine theme. Matt Chase naked. Yep.

Every Friday her sisters and sisters-in-law all congregated at one of their homes without husbands and children and had Martini Friday. Sometimes, usually during the summer it would be Margarita Friday instead but the idea was to gather, blow off the week, eat tasty food and have some drinks.

Tate changed and started the broiler before grabbing the ingredients she'd need from the fridge and cabinets. She loved the time just before people came over. That effort in preparing things for others, in sharing her food with them, in making her house comfortable and inviting.

Once she'd made the salad and pulled out the mini appetizers she'd prepared the night before, she dropped the chicken onto the broiler and moved into the living room to light candles.

PJ Harvey on the stereo singing about New York City made Tate sway a bit as she took the glasses from the cabinet and put them on a tray. It'd been a while since she'd had a date over for dinner. Cooking for dates was an odd thing. Some men liked it and enjoyed it but others, well their feelings about her weight transferred onto any event with food and made her feel self-conscious. She hated that. Her father made her feel that way and she didn't want anyone else to ever do that to her again.

She'd known why Anne got so angry earlier. They all knew Tate had continually re-directed his attention onto herself so her siblings could be spared their father's emotional abuse and Tim had done the same with the physical abuse. Her siblings were fiercely protective of each other and most especially her over her weight. It was a thing, a wound they all shared because of how cruel her father had been about it. While Tate truly wasn't bothered by it most of the time, they all took great umbrage when anyone ever made a flip or unkind remark, even Tate herself.

Talking on the porch lifted her out of her thoughts, she greeted her sisters with a smile.

℘

Like he did every Friday, Matt got together with his brothers at The Pumphouse for a few games of pool. He was the last single brother, a fact that every woman in town seemed to take up as a challenge. Free beers came his way multiple times a night, women traipsed past and bent over with come hither looks.

"I hate to admit it, but all this is tiring." He took a shot and missed.

Shane chuckled. "I figured it'd be hard on the last single Chase brother."

"Well, and now that Liv is pregnant, it's like blood in the water. Women not only throwing themselves at me but wanting to talk about babies too."

"Let yourself be caught then," Kyle said, grabbing one of the beers that'd been sent over.

"Hey, I will when it's the right woman."

"The right woman isn't gonna send over a beer and lean over so you can see her hoo ha," Shane grumbled.

Marc laughed. "What was that Daddy said back last year? Something about cookies? You hang out much at the Honey Bear lately?"

"Hardy har har. Speaking of cookies, do any of you know Tate Murphy?"

"Tim was in my year. Nice enough, I think. He was out a lot. He's a plumber here in town now. Damned good one. You know those roots on that oak in our backyard? Totally screwed up our laundry room plumbing. He came in and fixed it all. Nathan, he's one of the younger ones, he teaches at the high school with Maggie. You should ask Momma, she knows all that stuff." Kyle studied the table before taking a shot.

"Why?" Shane looked at his brother across the table.

"You know I helped out the other day when Charlie hit her? She sent me some cookies and I went in to thank her today. She's sweet. I was just wondering about her. Seems silly that in a small town I don't know someone so close to my age."

"I doubt she moves in the same circles."

"What's that supposed to mean, Marc?"

Marc drew back, surprised at the edge in Matt's voice. "Nothing. She's just not at the Tonk that I've ever seen, or here. Never seen her at the places we seem to hang out. So it's not a stretch to think she moves in different circles. What's your problem? She do or say something to upset you?"

"No. No, I'm sorry. I just took it the wrong way."

"Like how?" Marc leaned on his cue.

"She's, well she's sort of heavyset and if I remember correctly, Tim always had messed up clothes and was working on the side."

"You thought I meant since she was fat and poor she wasn't our kind?" Marc narrowed his eyes at his brother and Kyle put a hand on Marc's arm.

"No, I think Matt likes her and is feeling protective of her. Like you'd be of any one of your friends. Right?" Kyle asked Matt.

Matt nodded. "And she's not fat. Don't say that."

"I was being sarcastic." Marc sent him an agitated glare.

Matt put his cue away. "Whatever. I need to go. I'll see you all on Sunday."

Shane frowned and motioned to Kyle and Marc to stay back while he followed Matt out the door.

"Hey, asshole, wait up," Shane called out and Matt stopped, his shoulders drooping.

"I want to go home. Why are you pestering me?"

"Take your attitude down a notch or five or I'll have to kick your punky ass, Matt. What's going on with you? You're all over Marc tonight."

"I'm just—I don't know what I am. I suppose I just felt bad for them all the sudden. The Murphys. Anyway, it's been a long week. I'm going to go talk to Momma and then go home. I'll see you later. I'm all right, really."

"You know where I am if you need me, okay?"

"Yeah. Thanks, Shane."

Shane squeezed his brother's shoulder and let him walk away.

Matt drove over to his parents' house. The lights were on so they were still up. He tapped on the back door and his mother looked out the window, frowning as she opened it.

"Well come on in, boy. Why did you knock?"

He kissed her cheek and waved to his father, who sat in the breakfast nook, a steaming cup of tea at his right hand and the newspaper spread on the table before him.

"I didn't want to barge in and wake the baby up. It's after nine."

She rolled her eyes. "Sit down. I just made some tea and got Nicky down. He loves being with his Nanna and Pops." She smiled at the mention of her grandson, who'd be turning a year old in just a few short months.

"Pretty soon you'll have another one to spoil." He grinned and she did too. His father chuckled as he put the newspaper aside to drink his tea and visit with his son.

"It's a happy time around here, isn't it? What brings you to my kitchen?" She poured him some tea and put a slice of coffee cake in front of him.

"Momma, do you know much about the Murphy family? Tate?"

She smiled, the way she did when she thought of someone she liked, and relief settled into him. "Tate's a sweetie pie. She was just telling me you and Shane helped her the other day after Charlie whacked her with his car. I tell you, I know it's a sin but I was relieved it was someone else's bad driving that got them in trouble for a change."

Wisely, Matt avoided his father's gaze so neither man would laugh. He knew his mother would pick up the story so he ate the cake and waited.

"Anyway, Tate and her sisters own the salon where I get my hair done. Liv goes there regularly and Maggie from time to time too. Anne, the sister, she does my hair but Tate does all that newfangled razor cut stuff and the color jobby with the aluminum foil strips." Polly shrugged. "She's a nice girl. All those kids turned out so well. Especially considering what they came from."

Edward sighed and patted his wife's hand.

"What do you mean?"

"The father, um, Bill, yeah that's right, total drunkard. Lazy fool. Those kids went hungry a lot, I think. We tried to think on ways to get them food but the father…" She shook her head. "Refused any so-called charity. We did manage to get the kids free lunch at school. That Tate, she's something else."

"Why do you say that?"

Her very perceptive eyes narrowed, honing in on him. "Why are you asking?"

"She sent me cookies today for helping her after the accident. I met her when I went to thank her. She seemed nice but I realized I didn't know much about her. Kyle suggested I ask you."

She harrumphed. "Tate Murphy is a nice girl, Matthew Sebastian Chase. She and her older brother are the ones who raised the rest of those children. Eight in all. The mother, she's worse than the father. Kept having 'em and running off again with some new man who blew through town. I saw Tate with babies on her hip when she was in kindergarten. They didn't have the same kind of child welfare services then. But from what I've seen and heard over the years, every single one of those kids went to college if they wanted to or some kind of trade school and they all pooled together to pay for it. Tate and Tim being the oldest have done the lion's share."

"How come I never saw any of this?" Matt felt shame that all this happened to people his age and he never knew.

"Oh, they lived over in the trailer park on Ash. Not like you had much call to get out that way. You were lucky children to have your lives free of that sort of thing." Polly clucked.

35

The other side of the metaphorical tracks. That part of town was ramshackle and dark. Not the tree-lined stately homes of his neighborhood or even the nice residential flavor of the majority of Petal. That side of town had more burnt out cars and trucks up on blocks than oak trees.

He stayed and visited with his parents for a while longer and went home. But Tate's wide, friendly smile stayed with him even after he'd turned off the lights.

Chapter Four

Matt saw her everywhere once he'd actually noticed her the first time. That bright shock of white-blonde hair was a beacon along with the vivid, colorful clothes she always wore.

Somehow, it fit and he loved the retro vibe it lent her. Quite often, she wore dresses that made him think of the fifties. Flared skirts and tight bodices in bright red or blue. Always shoes to match. The woman could probably give Cassie a run for her money in the shoe department.

Two weeks after he'd gone into her shop that first time, he saw her sitting on a bench at city hall. It was early May and the day was clear and warm. Her hair gleamed in the sunshine.

He plopped down on the bench next to her and began to unpack his lunch. "Hey there. This seat taken?"

Her surprised jump made him glad she wasn't eating or drinking anything after the first choking incident. "Hi. No. No, sit down. I was just having my lunch."

Looking between his sandwich and whatever the heaven-in-a-bowl she was eating, made his stomach growl. "What is that? Looks way better than a turkey sandwich."

She held out a forkful to him and without thinking he took it. Instantly, his taste buds lit as the flavor rushed into his mouth.

"It's green curry with tofu."

"That's tofu? No way. Tofu tastes like, well, nothing."

She laughed, that sweet, musical laugh. "Tofu will soak up the flavor of whatever you cook it with. This has garlic, basil, eggplant and tofu in it and I like to add mushrooms just because. The green curry is spicy and the coconut milk is sweet. All together it just works doesn't it?"

"Yeah. I'll never wrinkle my nose at tofu again."

She curled her lip at his sandwich. "Is that *pressed turkey*?" Her tone made it seem like he'd been eating dog poop.

"Um, I don't know?" He shrugged. "I get it at the market, in those baggies where the cheese is. Is it bad?"

"Tell me something, Matt Chase, does your mother ever serve turkey that tastes like that?"

He recoiled in horror. "Never!"

She handed him the curry. "Good Lord, eat this. And go to the deli to get your turkey there next time. You know what a tomato is right?"

Obediently he ate and nodded. "But it makes the sandwich soggy."

"Keep the slices in a separate baggie until you're ready to eat the sandwich." She peeled the bread and looked at him accusingly. "Is this processed cheese? The kind that comes in little individual plastic sleeves?"

"Yeah. Hey, I like that stuff!"

"No you don't."

She sounded so sure of it, he started to doubt himself. Instead, he ate the food she'd given him. "What are you going to eat?"

She pulled out another container and two small containers. "I have marinated tomatoes and mozzarella with crostini."

"Huh?" He leaned over and nearly drooled when she pulled the lid off the container and the scent of olive oil and basil hit him along with the sweet acid of the tomatoes. "No way."

Grinning, she popped a tiny ball of cheese into his mouth and he groaned. "You can't have it all but I'll share some of it. I usually give my leftovers to Beth. If she hunts you down later, don't blame me." She pulled several little toasts out of a paper sack. "This is crostini. Just little pieces of toasted bread with olive oil or even plain. You put things on it, olive spread, tomatoes, cheeses, that sort of thing. My brother William works at The Honey Bear. He bakes the bread and tempts me with it even though fresh sourdough bread is the last thing I need every day."

"I go in there all the time. I can't believe I haven't recognized him. Does he look like you?"

"He starts work at four in the morning and he's off by two most days. You wouldn't see him, he bakes in the basement. All of my brothers and sisters are redheads with green eyes except me and Nathan. Nate's got brown hair. William looks like a younger version of Tim, my older brother."

He'd started to chide her about the bread thing until she spoke about her coloring. He remembered back to his momma's comments about Tate's mother's behavior.

Tate cocked her head and he actually saw her openness evaporate. "Yes, I'm aware of my mother's reputation, it's well-deserved but you won't catch poor white trash by sharing a fork with me."

"Whoa!" The hurt in her words nearly made his eyes water. Putting the bowl down, he reached for her hand. "I would never think such a thing. Tate, I don't think that about you."

"I saw your face change when I described my coloring to you." She tried to remove her hand but he wouldn't let go.

"Yes. Yes, okay, I did think about what I'd heard about your mother. But that has nothing to do with you. I don't even know your mother. For all I know, your dad has blond hair and blue eyes."

"Both my parents are redheads with green eyes, Matt. Don't think everyone in the world didn't notice me and Nathan and that we don't look a damned thing like my father. Don't think my father failed to notice and make us pay."

He stilled. "What do you mean?"

She began to pack her things up. "I need to get back to work."

Reaching out, he touched her arm and she stopped, looking into his eyes. "Wait. I'm sorry. I didn't mean to pry. If you leave I have to give your food back." He grinned tentatively and she snorted.

"Ugh, another man after my food. I have to beat you all off with a stick. Really, it's difficult to be objectified that way."

He laughed but he saw her humor as a way to deflect the conversation away from her comment about her father.

They stayed for another twenty minutes or so before she had to get back to the salon.

"I'll walk back with you. I need to get to work too. I can't believe we work across the street and I've never really hung out with you before." He helped her pack up. "Wow, what is this little lunchbox thing?"

"Cool isn't it? It's a Mr. Bento. I got it at this cookware store in Atlanta a few months back."

They walked companionably through the early May afternoon toward their end of town.

"I take it you like to cook?"

She nodded. "It's a great stress reducer. It's a way I can do something for my family."

"So you cut their hair and make them curry?" He grinned, liking that a lot.

"I do. Although Anne is really good with hair too. We're all pretty handy in the kitchen but it sort of turned into my place to be the house everyone comes to for dinner." And they all knew her cupboards would never be bare, ever. Once she'd moved out, that was her promise to herself and she'd kept it. No one she loved would ever be hungry if she could help it.

"Do you do men's hair? I think I need a cut." Absently, he ruffled a hand through his hair and a surge of giddiness rushed through her. Thirty-one years old with a crush, wasn't that special.

"We don't get a lot of men in the shop. Men in Petal tend toward the barber shop on First. But we get a few and I'd be happy to do you. Um, do your hair that is." She blazed bright red.

He laughed. "You blush easily don't you?"

"It's a curse of very pale skin I suppose." They stopped just outside the salon. "Give a call to check the schedule, I'll be glad to fit you in and trim you up." She brushed the hair away from his neck and tsked. "And I'll get your neck too."

"Okay, I'll do that." He paused before waving and crossing. On the other side of the street he called out, "Thanks for the curry. I'll talk to you soon, Tate."

"Hoo boy," she mumbled, watching him as he went back into the stationhouse.

❧

Matt found himself in Tate's company several times a week.

He liked Tate Murphy a lot. Liked her cooking, liked her sense of humor, liked the shape of her eyes and the smattering of freckles on the apple of her cheeks. Her voice was low and scratchy, totally unique, just like the rest of her.

He found himself thinking about her when he wasn't with her and making excuses to try and bump into her around town.

About a month after that first lunch with Tate, Kyle had invited himself over to Matt's apartment with Nicholas and the three of them spent the afternoon watching NASCAR and building block towers. Nicholas was quickly approaching a year old and Matt had baby-proofed his living room and kitchen to make it safe for his nephew's presence. Still, the boy was fast as lightning.

Kyle jumped up to grab Nicholas when the doorbell rang. He opened it with Nicholas under his arm, laughing.

"Oh, I'm sorry. I thought this was Matt's apartment."

Matt perked up at the familiar voice. He looked around Kyle's body and saw Tate standing there holding a duffel. "It's my place. Kyle and Nicholas are hanging out today. Come on in."

She hesitated and Kyle stepped back, allowing Matt to take her arm and pull her inside before she could bolt.

"I, I'm sorry to interrupt. I was in the neighborhood and I remembered you saying you lived here." That pretty blush crept up her neck.

"You're welcome to visit any time. Is this a social call or...?"

Nicholas jumped out of Kyle's arms and before either of them could move, Tate had effortlessly dropped the duffel and grabbed Nicholas and held him to her. Face close to his, she grinned and kissed his nose. "Hey you, the ground is lots harder than you think. Let me help." She lowered him carefully but he didn't take his eyes from her. Instead, he held his hand up and took her finger, tugging her over to his block tower and began to babble about it.

Kyle's eyes widened as Tate sat down and began to babble back and forth with Nicholas and work on the tower.

"Not a social call, not purely," she said over her shoulder.

Matt stood still for a long moment, looking at this woman who took joy from building a tower with his nephew. She wasn't faking it to seem attractive to him, he'd seen that one and it burned him up every time. No, Tate Murphy genuinely liked Nicholas and was having fun with him. How cool was that?

"Can I get you something to drink? Oh and that's Nicholas there and his daddy, my brother Kyle. Kyle and Nicholas, this is Tate."

Kyle moved to the place where Tate sat with Nicholas and joined them. "Hi, Tate. Nice to meet you."

"I've heard a lot about you. Your mother and sister-in-law Liv come into my shop a lot. Sometimes Maggie too. And you, Mister, are a very good builder. I'm very impressed. I haven't built block towers in a few years and I'm a bit rusty, thank you for helping me."

Matt brought her a glass of lemonade and swallowed hard. Holy shit, yep, Tate was...well, yeah. He liked her. *Liked* her liked her. When did that happen?

"What were you doing 'round these parts?" Jealousy stabbed through Matt as Nicholas reached up and petted Tate's hair. "Not that I'm complaining, it's nice to see you."

"I was just at the assisted living house a few blocks away. I go on the first Sunday of the month with Anne and we do the ladies' hair. It's hard for them to get out like they want to, so we go to them. And the last several times we had lunch together you kept telling me you needed a haircut and as I was in the area and had my stuff with me, I thought I'd make a house call."

"You're good with kids and the elderly too? You're running an animal shelter at your house aren't you?" He grinned.

"I'm horrible with animals! We didn't have pets when I was growing up and I have to admit dogs scare me and cats don't seem to like me. I'm also a terrible housekeeper and I'm late all the time. I have many flaws." She laughed. "I can come by another time for the cut since you're busy."

"No. Please. Today is the first Sunday in over a month I've not been working or at someone else's house. The wives are all out baby shopping, that's why Kyle and Nicholas are here with me." Did he even breathe through any of that?

"Would you do my hair, too?" Kyle asked and Matt wanted to pop him one.

She stood. "Of course. When Nicholas is ready, you let me know. I do children's cuts too."

"You can do it today if you like. I mean, he needs it." Kyle picked Nicholas up.

"Oh no. There's no way I'd cut a baby's hair without his momma there. You'd be in big trouble with your wife, I'd wager, Kyle. But oftentimes, if it's a first cut, kids feel better in familiar places so I'd be happy to cut his hair at your house or wherever."

Abashed, Kyle smiled. "Yeah, you're probably right about Maggie. She's touchy about that sort of thing."

Tate pushed Matt toward a kitchen chair she'd placed by his window. "That's not touchy, silly. She's his mom, a first haircut is a milestone, she'd want to be there. I do love his hair, though. My nieces and nephew have red hair, too."

Matt allowed her to direct him into the chair and she put a fabric drape over him and one on the floor to catch the hair. He zoned out as she touched him.

"First thing, let me shave your neck." Gently, the clippers trimmed and shaved his neck. Her hands were gentle as she worked and the soft scent he'd come to recognize as uniquely hers wafted through the air.

She'd nearly finished with his cut when a group of women showed up at his door.

"I've come to gather my men," Maggie said, waltzing into the apartment, stopping when she caught sight of Tate. "Tate, how are you?"

His gregarious Tate suddenly got shy. "Hello, Maggie. I'm fine, just cutting Matt's hair. I should be going though."

She started to move away but Matt grabbed her arm. "No, not yet."

Kyle grinned at them both. "You said you'd cut my hair too."

Blushing, Tate cleared her throat, her eyes widening and looking to Maggie. "Well, I'm sure you'll want to be with your family now."

Maggie laughed. "Oh, hell no. I've been after him to get a trim for weeks. He goes to the barber shop and they always cut it too short and then he waits until it gets shaggy."

Liv came into the room with Marc and seeing Tate, she smiled. "Hey Tate. You do house calls?"

"Hello, Liv. I hear congratulations are in order." Matt noticed her shyness got even worse with Liv's presence. He wondered if it was that they used to date or if there was another story.

"Thank you." Liv touched her belly and then her hair. "I'm in dire need of a cut but I'm a total worry-wart about the chemicals and smell in salons."

"It's okay, I understand. I can come by your place if you'd like. That way you wouldn't have to worry."

"Really? Oh that would be fabulous. Do you have time today?"

Tate blushed and nodded.

Matt just watched the interplay and let it settle in. He'd been startled by the revelation but now, he realized, it'd been happening since that first visit at her salon. Damn, she was a good woman, a genuinely nice person.

She ended up cutting Kyle's, Marc's and Liv's hair as well as giving Nicholas a trim. Maggie sat and watched the whole thing and Matt knew he'd hear from his sisters-in-law after Tate left.

"I should go. I'm having dinner with my family tonight." Tate cleaned up, aided by Matt.

"Ah. I was going to see if you wanted to have dinner with me."

She froze, blushing again. The best thing about her was that he could tell what she was feeling by her skin tone.

"I'll be at our bench tomorrow. You can have lunch with me then."

He pulled his wallet out and her eyes widened again. "How much do I owe you?"

"Do you think I go door to door hustling haircuts on the weekend for extra cash?" Her hands fell to her hips.

"I...uh, no. But you're a hairdresser, you performed a professional service. I certainly don't think you'd do five haircuts for free." Matt looked to Maggie, who shrugged, also uncertain how to proceed.

It was Liv who broke the stalemate by shoving money into Tate's hand. "Shaddup. Take the money. I need you to come and do my hair in six weeks at my house and Marc's too while you're at it. I feel loads better already. You're a whiz with the scissors. If Kyle did your lawn or Marc designed a workout, they'd expect to be paid too."

Tate nodded shortly and put the money in her pocket. "Right then. Listen, I was just in Atlanta to see my brother and sister last weekend. Have you been to Lullaby Rose?"

Liv shook her head.

"I went in to get some stuff for my niece, she's turning three. Anyway, they're having a huge sale right now. I know you were out today but they have a lot of great stuff. It's near the convention center. I'm sure they have a website too."

Liv's eyes lit up and Maggie leaned in. "They have boy stuff too?"

"Oh yeah. Newborn to age six. All sorts of stuff."

Matt hefted her duffel when she readied to leave. "I'll walk you out."

"Okay then." Getting to her knees she accepted a hug from Nicholas. "I'll see you later, Nicholas." And said goodbye to everyone else.

At her car, Matt tossed the duffel into the passenger seat. "Thanks for today." He touched his hair and she shrugged.

"No problem. I'll see you tomorrow."

He'd wanted to try and smooch up on her but she got into the car before he could make a move. All he could do was wave as she pulled away from the curb.

Back inside, he moved to the couch. "Before anyone asks, yes, I'm into Tate. She seems utterly clueless though."

"Into? Yeah, that's a mild word for a man who stared at her like he wanted to devour her." Liv chuckled.

"She's not your usual type, Matt." Maggie bounced Nicholas

on her knee.

"What do you mean?"

"Stop being so damned defensive about her already," Marc grumbled. "She's *not* your usual type. She's a very nice woman, no doubt. But," he shrugged, "she's not the perky cheerleader beauty queen you normally date."

"What was that thing about the money?" Kyle asked.

Liv snorted. "You guys all grew up so sheltered. Tate Murphy is a hardscrabble girl. She came up the hard way. Struggled, worked for everything she has. She's defensive because of what she comes from."

"And how do you know? You grew up pretty well."

"I did, yes. And I'm lucky. Tate's sister-in-law Susan was tight with my sister. When they ran wild together anyway. Susan mellowed long before my sister did. Anyway, I know Susan pretty well and through her, I know a bit about the Murphys. It's going to be hard for you to get her to let you in, Matt. She's been hurt, a lot. And, I'm going to say it because it's my place to say things everyone is thinking but no one says—the looks thing is going to be a problem."

"What looks thing?" Matt thundered.

Liv waved it away. "I've known you a long time, Matthew. Don't play games. You go out with women who are drop-dead beautiful. Even I was intimidated when we dated. She's a beautiful person, that goes without saying, but she's not like the others."

"Are you saying she's ugly? Because that's fucked up, Liv, in addition to being untrue."

Liv snorted and put her hand on Marc's arm to keep him from speaking. "*I'm* not saying she's ugly. I know her. Not as well as I'd like to, she seems much more reserved around me than with other people. But enough to know I think she's beautiful. But here's what they're going to say, Matt—she's short and fat and from the wrong side of town. She's after your money and your name. You're tall, handsome and you come from money and an influential family." Liv shrugged.

"You have to be prepared for it, Matt. You have to protect her and yourself by accepting it up front and understanding how to deal with it. If you mean to make something with her, you're going to have a lot of hurdles. Other people may pretend that's not a problem but I'm not other people and I love you too much not to say what everyone is thinking."

Marc chuckled. "My fragile flower. So shy."

"I never thought of it that way. Well, I don't care what people think. I only care what I know. All my life people have just assumed I'm shallow. Kyle, he's the sensitive one, Shane is the gruff one, Marc's the happy-go-lucky one and I'm the pretty one no one thinks much of. I've gone out with dozens of women. I've been able to have a decent conversation with maybe three and only one has ever had the same feeling about family I have. I've gotten to know Tate over the last few months, this isn't sudden. She's the one. She doesn't judge me, she doesn't look at me and think about how much money I might inherit or how much my family name can do for her. She doesn't look at me and think that grabbing the last Chase bachelor would be a feather in her cap. She just sees Matt. No one else does. Do you know how special that is?"

Marc looked at Liv and then back to his brother, nodding. "I do. If you want her, you know you have our help and support."

"You know Momma will be in your corner. If anyone says a word about it in her presence they'll rue the day." Kyle and Maggie looked to him. "I'm looking forward to getting to know

Tate and making her part of our family. You've got our support."

Matt looked at them, the people he loved and smiled. "Thank you. Looks like I might just have a job and a half ahead of me. Good thing I've never shied away from a challenge."

"That's putting it mildly." Kyle winked.

Chapter Five

"Are you absolutely sure you want to do this?" Beth looked to Tate as they stood just outside the trailer.

"Sure? Fuck no. I *know* I don't want to do this. But Jill and Jacob are in there and they need our support. If Mom and Dad don't sign those papers, it'll be hard for the kids to get their loans. We can pay for most of it but without those loans, it's awfully hard. Plus, damn it, with their signatures they can keep getting state grants too. They deserve at least that from those two worthless assholes. So we do this once a year and thank the heavens it's just that rare an occurrence." Tate took a steadying breath and reached out to Anne on one side and Beth on the other. It fell to them because Tim, William and Nathan couldn't be in the same room with their father without violence breaking out. They all played to their strengths and worked together. Dealing with their parents was her cross to bear.

The door opened up and Jill stood there, relief on her face. "Hi guys, come on in." Her eyes sparked a warning and Tate steeled herself for the inevitable.

Once she walked up and through the creaky door, the assault of her entire childhood plagued her like it always did. The cloying stench of stale sweat, cheap perfume and alcohol assaulted her. God, she hated that smell.

Her mother raised a hand in halfhearted greeting from her place on the tattered sofa. Tina Murphy had a drink in the other hand. Her hair was currently platinum-blonde with three inches of red growout at the roots. No matter that her daughters were excellent hairdressers, no, Tina had killed her own hair with repeated home dye jobs that rendered it to straw.

Bracing herself, she bent to kiss her mother's cheek. "Hey, Mom."

"Hey, honey. I like that color on you." In her own way, Tina was closest to Tate. What passed for love in Tina's world was a scarcity but she did seem to care about Tate when she could be bothered to come home.

"Too bad orange isn't slimming. Those shoes are hideous. Trying to take the focus off your fat ass? You're late as usual, Tate. Stop at a drive-thru on your way over? Let's eat, we don't know when your mother will decide to cat off somewhere else." Her father's words had already taken on a heavy slur.

Jacob started to speak but Tate shook her head once, hard. If anyone engaged with their father, it would make matters worse. If you just ignored him, he gave up after a while. Or he passed out. Either way, he'd shut the fuck up before she gave in to her urge to smack the shit out of him with a frying pan.

"Good evening, Dad." She walked past him toward the tiny eating area. Her mother may have a lot of faults but when she concentrated for long enough she was a pretty good cook.

It was just a matter of holding out through dinner. Just finish, make nice and get the hell out of there before anyone cried.

"Did they sign the papers?" she asked Jill in an undertone.

Jill nodded imperceptibly.

Only one more year.

"Don't pass the potatoes by lard ass. I told you to make her a salad, Tina."

"Bill, shut the hell up already."

Tate drank her tea and kept her head down. Finally, after bickering back and forth, her father shut up. She didn't bother eating, it would only prolong the evening.

After strained small talk they all made an exit.

"Come back to my place?" Beth hugged Tate tight.

Tate shook her head and hugged Anne, Jill and Jacob too. "I need to be alone for a while. Shake this off. I'm not good company."

"Yes you are. Honey, don't do this alone." Anne kissed her forehead.

"Look, I give you all most of myself but this is mine. I'm going to go and eat dinner. Alone. Please."

"We're going to stay at William and Cindy's tonight. We still on for breakfast tomorrow before Jacob and I go back?" Jill asked.

Tate nodded. "Of course." She needed to be alone, damn it. Quickly, she got into her car and headed back into town.

At The Sands, Ronnie was there with a smile and a cup of coffee, ushering her to a corner booth. It was already half past eight on a Sunday night so the place was pretty uncrowded.

"Evening, Tate."

"Hey, Ronnie." Tate opened her menu.

"Hey, fancy seeing you here."

She looked up into Matt Chase's face and only barely resisted taking a long glance down the rest of him. His face was enough of a treat. Made her feel tingly when all she'd felt just moments before was numb.

"Can I join you? I've been on a call. Warren and Pearl Jervis's place. I wish they'd leave each other, but they won't. He set fire to their couch tonight. Made me miss dinner at my folks'."

"Sometimes it's because they don't know any other way. Other times, it's because they don't give a shit about anyone else and can't be satisfied until they bleed their misery on you."

"Wow, sounds like there's a story there. I'm sorry for bringing you down. You can tell me. Or, I promise to entertain you with happy stories if you let me sit with you."

She rolled her eyes and laughed. "Sure, have a seat."

Instead of sitting across from her, he slid into the booth beside her, stretching out his long legs next to hers.

"I'm absolutely convinced that Polly Chase will have a plate set aside for you in the oven as we speak," she said dryly to hide the tremor working through her at his nearness.

He grinned. "Probably. But I'd rather be here with you."

She narrowed her eyes at him but Ronnie came to take their order. "I'll have the roasted chicken with the rice and a salad. Vinegar and oil please, Ronnie."

"Give me the pork chops and mashed potatoes and a salad with ranch, and a beer."

"Oh yeah, that sounds excellent. Beer for me, too, please."

Ronnie smiled at them both and sauntered back to put their order in.

"Rough night?" Tate looked at him, liking the way his nose looked from the side.

"Why do you say that?" Matt asked warily.

"Because you had to go on what amounted to a domestic call, which can't be much fun. But you're here and avoiding your mother's cooking, which I hear is legendary. Is something up?"

He chuckled and took a long pull off the beer Ronnie dropped off along with the salads. "Polly is a mighty fine cook, yes. And I don't know how Shane does it. These domestic calls are awful. I don't have to deal with them often but when I do, it's hard to take, you know?"

"Yes, I do know."

He turned and their faces were just inches apart. She could see the beginnings of a beard on his cheeks and chin.

"Too close to home?"

"I really don't want to talk about that right now. Until about five minutes ago, I was having a very crappy night. It's looking up so don't screw with that."

"Tell me about your night and why it's been so bad."

"Dinner with my parents."

Matt nodded, wanting to know more. He'd only heard bits and pieces around town and from his mother. He knew the old man drank and the mother kept running off.

"I won't pretend that I don't know a little bit about your history. That's not who I am and it doesn't seem like who you are either. He been drinking?"

"Is that a rhetorical question? I'm sorry. I shouldn't be disrespectful of him. And it's not just him." She shook her head and waited while Ronnie put the food onto the table.

"Once a year I have to endure dinner with them. It's for my youngest brother and sister. Because they're still young, they need my parents' signature on their federal financial aid forms. We pay for most everything, my siblings and I. But it's expensive and they can get loans at reduced interest and grants. Anyway, it's just once a year. I go over there to check on him, my dad, every month or so but dinner there is just the worst. I sit and don't eat, for an hour, and we all dash out the back door and run for it."

"You don't eat?"

"So, how did you end up as a firefighter anyway?" she asked with a grin as she changed the subject.

He allowed it, for the time being. "I considered being a cop like Shane but the police academy was not my cup of tea. One of the instructors there suggested I try firefighting instead. I did." He shrugged. "I like it and the people of Petal. Well, most of them anyway. It's nice to find something that makes you feel fulfilled you know?"

"Yeah, I do know. When I first got out of high school, I did all sorts of odd jobs to pay the bills. Tim and I got an apartment in town, big enough for everyone. After a time, I got into beauty school and I realized I'd found what I was good at. It isn't police work or anything, but I like making people feel better about themselves. So many women have crappy lives or bad days or never get a chance to feel pretty or special. It's amazing what a bit of hair color and a nice cut can do. Make you walk out of the salon like you're on air." She smiled as she said it and Matt felt it like a blow to his gut.

"You have such a pretty smile."

She blushed charmingly. "Thank you."

They finished up and he ordered a slice of pie.

"I should go. I have an early breakfast with my family tomorrow morning. It was nice having dinner with you, Matt." She scooted out of her side of the booth and stood.

"Wait, have some pie with me."

"Oh, I can't."

"Can't? You allergic to peaches? If so they've got cherry and lemon meringue too." He grinned.

"No, I can't do pie. The crust goes straight to my butt and it's big enough as it is." She laughed but it sounded brittle.

"Tate, I happen to like your butt. In fact, it's pretty darned stellar. Come on. I know you want to," he sang out softly. He loved her shape, soft and lush, all curves and dips.

"Look, I have bad enough self control as it is, don't tempt me," she whispered and he stood. Thank goodness she had on some spiky heels or he'd have towered over her.

"It's just pie. It's supposed to be tempting." He grinned.

"I said no! It's easy for you. Stop it. I'm not laughing." The vehemence of her voice was laced with something else, pain and shame. Matt did not like the way it sounded one bit.

Tate let out a surprised gasp when Matt stepped to her, banding her waist with his arm, hauling her close. "Let me tempt you with something better then," he said in a near growl, so low it strummed along her spine. Her nipples pebbled against the front of her blouse and every other part of her called to attention. The heat of him buffeted her, nearly made her sway with want.

"Wh-what would that be?" Confusion swallowed her. What was he doing? This felt distinctly sexual and even more mutual. But it couldn't be. Matt Chase could not be...holy shit was that his cock poking into her belly?

"...a movie? Watch it at my place? Your place? Any place?"

"Huh?" God, he'd been speaking and she missed three quarters of it. The grin he sent her in response was so wicked an involuntary moan slipped from her lips.

"Would you like to come back to my apartment now? Have a drink or kiss? A lot?"

"Don't tease me like this, it's not nice." She tried to push away from him but he wouldn't let her go.

"I'm not teasing you, Tate. God, you have no idea how much I want you." He rolled his hips. "Here's a little clue though."

"I don't know."

"I do. Come on. Your place. Your rules. I promise to behave. Or well, to not push but I don't want to leave your company just yet and I'd really like to be alone with you." His lips skimmed over hers briefly and her resistance melted.

He reached into his pocket and tossed a wad of cash onto the table before all but pulling her outside into the warm June air.

At her car he stopped and spun her into his embrace, watching the way her skirt swirled around her legs. "I love this dress. And this color, it reminds me of orange sherbet. I do so love to eat orange sherbet."

She swallowed and felt like Alice fallen down the rabbit hole. Was Matt Chase rubbing his cock on her and inviting her to make out? She must have hit her head or something. It had to be a dream.

"I...this is a bad idea. You can't really want to hang out with me. You just feel guilty or something. Why would you want me like this?"

Matt exhaled in frustration. His damned cock was so hard it throbbed. It sure as hell didn't feel guilt. He wanted to fuck her so badly he was just barely holding himself together. Grinding his cock into her body, he felt triumphant when her eyes partially closed with pleasure. "I want to. I feel several things, Tate. Turned on. Hot for you. Desperately in dire need to kiss you. I want to touch you and be alone with you. I really truly do. Guilt isn't on the list of things I'm feeling for you." He grinned and she gave him a small smile in return.

She paused for long moments and finally nodded. "All right.

You can follow me home then."

He'd been driving to his parents' from that fucked up scene and her hair caught his eye as he'd spotted her through the windows at The Sands. A brief phone call to his mother to say he wasn't going to make it and he'd headed toward her. It wasn't like he could have done anything else. She called to him. Feeling like a teenager, Matt's hands shook as he drove to her house. Not a bad neighborhood. Not fabulous but solid working class. He knew which one was hers even before she turned into the driveway. The little bungalow was unique, just like she was.

He parked and tried not to shove her to her front door and pin her to the first available surface. Instead he took her hand, smiling at her that she'd waited at her car for him.

"It's a bit of a mess. I left in a hurry earlier today." She fumbled with the lock and her scent hit him hard when the door swung open. He couldn't even pinpoint what she smelled like, it wasn't perfume, she seemed too much a ball of raw energy to take the time to dab a bit of scent behind her ears. It reminded him of earth, not dirt, not musk, but vibrant, essential, heady.

"I like it. It feels like you in here. Colorful." He looked around and took the place in. Bright framed prints hung on her walls. "Frida Kahlo right?" He motioned toward one of the prints.

She nodded with a smile. "I love her stuff. Her husband, Diego Rivera got more attention but I think her art is startling and disturbing as well as just plain gorgeous."

"I don't know much about art. Do you know Cassie? Shane's wife? I think you'd like her. Your tastes are similar." If what Matt suspected about Tate's childhood was correct,

59

Cassie's experience as a victim's advocate might be really helpful as well. If anyone could understand Tate's perspective, Cassie would.

"I don't. I mean, I've seen her around town. Who could miss her?"

"What do you mean?"

"Uh, hello? It's not like you can miss a nearly six foot tall woman who looks like Cassie. I'm as straight as they come and I think I have a crush on her."

Matt laughed. Cassie was startlingly beautiful but the woman he was with right then was a thousand times more precious and she didn't even know it. "She's a pretty woman, yes. I'm sure you'll meet her soon. Come and sit down here. I can't kiss you if you're all the way over there."

He plopped down onto her couch and she stopped, looking at him, surprised. "What?"

"Yeah, not so good with the woo am I? I'd love for you to come here and sit with me."

Tate didn't know quite what to do. Matt Chase flustered the hell out of her. A sense of unreality settled into her. The guy, the donut of her dreams sat on her couch and wanted to kiss her? Did she hear him right?

"Tate? Did I say something to upset you? I want more than a kiss." He stopped and shook his head. "What I mean is I want to take you out too. This isn't just some fun way to spend my Sunday. Although, I'm certainly enjoying being with you. God, I'm usually more smooth than this," he mumbled and she laughed, kicking off her shoes and moving to the couch.

"I don't know what to say."

Scooting so that his body pressed full against hers, he put a finger over her lips. "Then don't say anything just now. I really need to kiss you, Tate. So I'm gonna."

His hand slid up her arm and cupped her neck, holding her, tipping her chin up. Before she had much of a chance to register anything but the delicious heat of his palm, his lips found hers.

Slow. Incrementally building up the heat, he gently led her to open up to his tongue. She'd never been really crazy about kissing but she realized it was just that she'd never been kissed by someone who knew what he was about before. All the difference in the world lay right there.

He didn't jam his tongue in her mouth and down her throat, he teased her with it, tasted her, tickled her with the tip. His teeth joined the action, coming in to nip her bottom lip from time to time until she nearly panted with wanting him more.

The heat of his mouth moved from her lips, skating along her jaw to the hollow just below her ear. A gasp ripped from her gut when he sucked there, the wet, warm sensation shooting straight to her nipples and then to her pussy, flooding her with moisture.

Needing more of him, she adjusted, sliding her hands up into his hair.

Matt had never wanted a woman more than he did as the taste of her rushed through him. She was soft under his hands, smelled right, felt good. These little sounds kept coming from her, little moans and sighs of need, and it drove him crazy. He didn't want to scare her but if he didn't get inside of her sometime soon his cock would explode.

Before he knew it, her hands had slid from his hair to his chest and she was opening the front of his uniform shirt. Hesitantly but with some strength, she pushed him back enough to get on her knees and part the front of his shirt. When she leaned down to brush kisses over his collarbone before moving to flick a tongue over his nipples, he jumped, breathing her name like a prayer.

Her hair was like silk over his superheated skin. Needing to see it all, he reached back and undid the clasp holding it up. It tumbled down in a sweet-smelling wave.

When one of her hands slid down his belly and her nails scored over his cock he moved back into action.

He took her arms so he could see in her face. What greeted him, passion-glazed eyes and kiss-swollen lips, made him suck in a breath. Holy shit she was beautiful.

"Tate, I want you. Are you with me?"

Swallowing, she nodded before licking her lips.

"Bedroom?"

She stood, held out a hand and led him toward the back of the house. He felt her tremble a bit, but as he was shaking too, it was hard to tell where he began and she ended.

Her room was messy and it made him smile.

"God, I'm sorry. I...well it goes without saying I wasn't expecting to bring a man back here." She motioned toward her unmade bed and turned out the light he'd turned on.

For some reason, that comment only made him want her more.

"Good." He used his body to push her toward her bed until she fell back and looked up at him, her hair a brilliant corona around her head. "Tate, I want to see you." He turned on the bedside lamp before moving to unbutton the bodice of the dress she wore.

The blush was back and she put her hands over his, stilling them. "Turn the light off, please."

"But I won't be able to see you that way. Tate, I've been fantasizing nonstop about your body for weeks now."

"I can't. Matt, please."

Instead of turning the light off, he lay down on the bed and pulled her to him. "Tate, are you changing your mind about making love to me?" She shook her head but he saw the glimmer of tears in her eyes. "What is it, sweetness? Am I scaring you? Moving too fast?"

She buried her face in his neck and he burrowed through her hair to hold her. "I don't want you to see me naked."

"If you're not naked, how can I be inside you?" That's when it occurred to him he didn't have any condoms.

"Just leave the lights off!"

"Tate, I want to see you. Would you deny me that pleasure?" He pulled his head back to see her face, hoping she'd smile but he got confusion, anger and a bit of embarrassment too. What the fuck? "Tate? What is it?"

She pushed at him and jumped up, pacing in front of the bed. "I'm not one of the women you're normally with!"

"I know."

She stopped and sneered.

"I mean," he added quickly, "yes, you're not like them. And that's a *good* thing. Tate, you're important, special."

"Matt," she sighed, sounding impatient. "Are you going to make me spell it out?"

"You'd better, sweetness, because I have no fucking idea what the issue is."

"Dolly, Melanie, Lisa, Kelly—what do these things have in common and what do I not have that they do?"

"They're vapid and shallow and you're not?" Standing and going to her, he kissed her lips quickly, tossing his shirt to one side blindly.

"Okay, well, you have a point there. Although what the hell

were you doing with them if so?" The air left her lips in a soft whoosh when he pushed her gently back down to the bed.

"Well you have a point there too. We can talk about the ramifications of that later because it's totally getting in the way of me putting my cock into your body. And speaking of that, we're not getting naked again why?"

"Because you go out with women who are drop-dead gorgeous and I am not! They're all tall and thin and *cheerleaders*. I am, aside from having breasts and a vagina, nothing like them."

He tried not to laugh, he really did but she was hilarious.

"What are you laughing at?"

He rolled and pinned her to the bed with his body, raining kisses down her chest, over the fabric of her dress. Pulling her skirt up, he traced the soft skin of her thighs with his fingertips.

"I'm laughing at you, Tate Murphy. I've never heard anyone but Maggie say cheerleader like it was some sort of disease. Frankly, I find it hard to find fault with women jumping around in tight sweaters and short skirts but I don't think it has a damned thing to do with why I'm dying here for you and not with anyone else. I'm here because *you're* here. I don't want them, I want you. I want to see your body, I think you're beautiful."

"I can't concentrate with the lights on."

There was so much panic and emotion in her voice he let it go. Reaching out, he turned out the light.

"Better?"

"Yes."

He found her mouth again and she relaxed, melting into him, hooking one of her thighs around his ass, arching her back to bring her pussy into contact with his cock.

Busy hands found the buttons on her bodice and made quick work of them, exposing her bra to him. He wished he could see more in the dim light that came from the open bedroom door but there'd be time for that later.

There wasn't a catch between her breasts so he helped her to sit up to get the back hooks undone.

Sweet mercy, her breasts, even what he could see in the low light, were beautiful. Large, heavy, juicy, dark nipples.

While she sat up, he helped her get the dress off and tossed his pants, socks and boxers before returning to her. She'd slid under the sheets, which agitated him, but he began to really understand some of what Liv had said a few weeks before about what some people might think about Tate. Apparently Tate herself felt some of those things too. Well, that'd be next, showing her just how damned beautiful she was—cheerleader or not.

When their bodies came together, skin to skin he thought he'd lose consciousness it was so deliriously good. Fuck! Condom.

"Tate, uh, I have a problem. *Shit!*" She grasped his cock, giving a few slow pumps with her fist.

"What is it?" She nibbled on his ear and he lost his train of thought for long moments until she smeared her thumb over the wet slit at the head of his cock.

"Condom. I don't have one. Please, please tell me you do." He caught a nipple between his lips, swirling his tongue around it.

"I, ohgod, I don't. I don't bring men back here for sex."

He rested his forehead on her chest a moment, disappointed but not in her comment that she didn't bring men back for sex. "Okay, well I'm not leaving to go get one either. We'll just work around it. We can do other things for tonight."

"Other things? Oh, yesss."

His fingers found her pussy, wet and swollen. He kicked back the sheets and kissed his way back and forth between her nipples as his fingertips teased around her swollen clit. She was slick and ready and he needed more.

Kissing a trail south, he marveled at the soft swell of her belly as he insinuated himself between her thighs. He felt her muscles tense but before she could object, he spread her labia and took a long, deep taste of her and they both sighed.

She was sweet and savory all at once. Her clit bloomed under his tongue and he realized he was quickly becoming addicted to making Tate feel good.

Tate could not believe she was in her bed with Matt Chase's mouth on her pussy. Naked. Naked! She wished it weren't so dark so she could see his body, she knew it would be gorgeous. She certainly hadn't had a complaint when she grabbed his cock and found him nice and thick.

No condom, fuckadoodledoo. She added a trip to the drugstore after breakfast to her mental to-do list. She wasn't sure there'd be a part two to this interlude but if fate was that kind to her again, she'd be ready.

Oh, almost there, just a bit... "*Fuck* me!" she exclaimed as he sucked her clit into his mouth and pressed two fingers into her pussy at the same time. Orgasm hit her hard, stealing all speech but a long hard exhale.

Moments later, he kissed the inside of her thighs and moved to lie beside her. "I'd love to fuck you, by the way," he murmured into her ear and she laughed.

"Sorry, I have a fuck habit. That's to say I say it too much."

"I haven't noticed it." He kissed her shoulder and she pushed him back and kissed down his chest.

"I've been trying to watch my mouth around you."

"Something I hope will end right about now," he groaned as her tongue traced his navel.

The man had the hardest, flattest belly she'd ever licked. He smelled so good she wanted to take a bite but resisted, being so close to his cock and all.

A cock that by any indicators she'd been acquainted with, was quite pleased at her presence. Especially when she ran the flat of her tongue across the head and around the crown.

Sliding her hair over his abdomen and thighs, she took him into her mouth—all she could—and pulled back only to suck him back inside again.

"Tate, oh, yeah, right like that. You're...holy...oh."

Triumph and pride bloomed within her. She'd reduced Matt Chase to incoherence. Her, Tate Murphy, the girl most likely to not be remembered by anyone. It wasn't like she'd given a thousand blow jobs or anything, she just wanted to please him and she couldn't get enough of him.

She'd never considered fucking without a condom but damn she wanted him badly. Still, she'd seen the results of thinking with one's pink parts. Tate did not want to be end up like her mother. Or her father, whoever the hell he was.

Matt's thigh bunched and flexed beneath her palm as she loved him with her mouth. Her nails lightly traced his balls as they pulled tight against his body. He made a small sound at the back of his throat and then said her name as he came.

Sometime right after, he pulled her up and encircled her with his arms. "Condoms. Next time there'll be condoms."

She laughed, totally happy.

Until her phone rang. She picked up the receiver and looked at the caller ID window. "I'm sorry, it's one of my sisters." She hit the on button. "Yes?"

"Are you all right?"

"Beth, I'm busy. I'll talk to you tomorrow. I'm fine."

"You know, you can't run off after these dinners, the twins blame themselves."

"Beth, I don't want to talk about this right now." She sat up and grabbed a robe from the nearby chair and pulled it on as she stood and headed for the hall.

"Tate, you take the brunt of dealing with them and then you run away. We all feel guilty about that. Why don't you let us help?"

"Beth! For fuck's sake! Let it go. You can't have everything. I give you all ninety-nine percent but I'm allowed to have my own feelings about dealing with them. I wouldn't do it if I didn't want to. I'll see you in the morning but I'm warning you, don't bring it up again."

"Tate..."

"Good night, Beth. I'm hanging up now. I love you." She hit the off button and turned off the ringer. When she turned, Matt stood there in the doorway to her bedroom and yep, he looked better naked than in clothes.

"Is everything all right?"

"Yes. Family." She shrugged. "I expect you know what I mean."

He moved to her, pulling her into his arms. "I do indeed. Can I help?"

She laughed, tossing the phone on the couch. "I think you've done your part in my stress relief."

"Well, come back to bed, I've got a few more tricks up my

sleeve."

"Sweet talker."

He'd stayed until nearly two but as both of them needed to be up early, she talked him into going home. Not that it stopped her from sleeping on the side of the bed he'd been in, loving his scent.

Not only that, but he'd asked her out on a real date for the following Saturday night and she'd agreed.

She headed into town to the Honey Bear where her siblings were all meeting for breakfast before the twins headed back to Atlanta. They were taking summer classes to finish school early.

Ignoring Beth's frown, she kissed everyone and took the seat they'd been saving. A full house, so full they'd had to push two tables together to fit all eight siblings, two spouses and four children.

They had coffee and talked around the dinner the night before. Things had eased up by the time they'd all eaten and headed their separate ways. Anne, Beth and Tate all walked to the shop to open up.

"I had sex with Matt Chase last night."

Anne, who'd been cleaning her scissors, looked up, surprised. "You did?" Plopping into Tate's chair, she put her hands on her lap. "Do tell. And don't dream of skipping a single detail."

"What's going on?" Beth wandered past.

"Tate was just going to give me all the details of her sexual encounter with Matt Chase last night."

"What? That's what busy meant? Shit, I'd have hung up on

me too. Tell us."

"I didn't hang up on you. I told you I was hanging up."

Beth rolled her eyes. "Details I don't care about. Matt Chase, naked, in your bed? That I care about."

Tate made sure the place was empty and told them all the details, including their plans for a date that Saturday.

"It's about time. He's only been looking at you like a hungry puppy for the last month."

Tate looked to Anne. "What do you mean?"

"Tate, you're so clueless. He shows up where you're going to be as many days a week as he can. You two have lunch together what? Three days a week? He calls here just to say hey. You make enough food for two when you bring your lunch. He likes you. And that's no surprise to me."

"He's out of my league, Anne. So far out of my league I've made a pact not to think about it overmuch until it comes crashing down around my ears."

Anne looked angry. "Damn you, Tate. Why do you have such a low opinion of yourself? Why do you let Dad make you feel this way?"

"Okay, we're done now. I have a client in about five minutes." Tate shooed them all away from her station and looked out the window at the fire station across the street, wondering if Matt was inside.

Chapter Six

"Beth, I'm throwing myself on your mercy. Please go shopping with me." Tate showed up at the front desk at closing time on Thursday night.

"Come to my parlor said the spider to the fly." Beth chuckled. "You're in luck. You don't even have to go shopping. I know how much you hate it so I went shopping last night and picked up a few things for your date. Come to my apartment and try them on."

They drove over to Beth's place and Tate sucked it up and tried on the outfit, undergarments and shoes her sister had bought.

"Since you're going to the Tonk, I thought this might suit best." Beth held up a black dress with a full skirt, covered in red roses. The bodice was tight, with three-quarter sleeves. "I think it'll give you lots of movement when you're dancing. And let's face it, Tate, no one dances like you."

Tate liked the dress immediately and even got over feeling exposed by the deep vee of the neckline. It didn't make her look like a super model or anything, but it showcased her better features and camouflaged her not so good ones—namely her thighs. With a pair of pretty heels and her hair done just right, she'd do in a pinch. Okay, more than that, she looked pretty and what woman didn't like to look pretty?

"Thank you, Beth. It's perfect."

Beth grinned. "It does look really lovely on you. By the way, we're going to the Tonk Saturday night too."

"We?"

"Me, Nathan, Anne and Royal. What? You think we'd just throw you to the wolves over there?"

There was a reason the Murphys did their drinking and dancing at Reba's over in Riverton instead of The Tonk. The Tonk wasn't their place, was generally filled with people who had made fun of them when they were younger.

"Well, I could pretend to be annoyed but you'd see through me. Thank you." Tate hugged Beth. "I appreciate the back-up."

"Tate, I don't say this enough, but I've always got your back. It's not that I feel like I owe you for raising me. You're my sister and my best friend and I love you. We're family and that's what family does. If anyone says one wrong thing I'm planting a boot in their ass."

Tate laughed. "Well, I'd pay to see that one."

ॐ

"You ready for your date tomorrow?" Marc took his shot as he spoke to his brother.

"It's not like I've never been on a date before."

"Not with *the one* you haven't. Liv's all worked up." Marc grinned and his eyes gravitated to his wife who sat at the front of The Pumphouse at her usual table.

"You shouldn't bring her. It's smoky in there. It's not like you have to protect me from Tate Murphy. She's barely five feet tall." Matt chuckled.

"You say that as if I have a choice in what my beautiful wife does. She assures me we'll get a table near the back doors which are open during the summer."

"They're all planning on something," Shane rumbled as he looked at the table.

"Count on it. Maggie's the ringleader no doubt. She wants to be sure we get there early so we can welcome Tate properly. And she warned me about *those stuck up bitches* I used to date and how I'd better be sure to make Tate feel more welcome than she felt." Kyle grinned.

"For a little thing, your woman is scary."

Kyle laughed. "And now yours is even smaller. What's Tate? Like five-one?"

"She claims five-two but I think she's fudging a half an inch. There's a lot to her."

"Well, I'm looking forward to getting to know her better. I have to say I heartily approve from my time with her at your place a few weeks back. When are you going to tell Momma and Daddy?" Kyle asked.

"I'm trying to get her to come to dinner on Sunday. I figured I'd talk to Momma tomorrow afternoon. I need to pick up some stuff they're donating to the firefighter's auction. I'm sure adding another plate won't be a big deal."

Marc laughed. "No big deal? Yeah, you keep thinking that."

ॐ

Matt couldn't believe his eyes when Tate opened her door. She stood there in a black dress covered in big red roses. Bright red lips, silver hoops in her ears. She'd done something to her hair so that it hung in smooth, pale waves around her face. She looked like a fifties movie star.

"Holy shit. Tate, you look gorgeous."

She blushed and he couldn't help but kiss her on her neck.

"Thank you. It's Beth's doing. She picked it out. You look very nice too. I haven't seen you dressed for dancing."

He kept an arm around her waist and pressed another kiss just beneath her ear, up the side of her face and over her brow. "You taste good."

"My, you're very fancy with the compliments. By the way, a few of my siblings are going to be at The Tonk tonight. I hope you don't mind."

He escorted her to his truck and helped her in.

"Of course I don't. My brothers and sisters-in-law will be there too. They're all anxious to get to know you."

"Yeah, 'cause that won't make me nervous or anything."

"They're all very nice people. You already know Liv and Maggie."

"Sort of. It's not the same, working for someone. It's not like I'm friends with them or anything."

He nodded, chewing over that mentally as he drove. "Well, okay, if you say so. It's hard for me to know and all, they're part of my life so I just think of them as friends."

"Liv was your girlfriend too, right? For awhile a few years back?"

He laughed. "Yes. Odd isn't it? She married my little brother and she's going to have his baby in September."

"Odd, yeah that's a word for it."

"Does it weird you out?" Admittedly, he hadn't thought of that, of how the woman he'd want to be with would feel about Liv.

"Well, I don't really have a place to be weirded out. It's just a date."

"Tate, it's not *just* anything. I don't want you to feel uncomfortable being with me when we're out. There's nothing between me and Liv, hasn't been for years now. She's one of my best friends and my brother's wife, that's it."

"This *conversation* is making me uncomfortable."

He laughed. He liked it when she got prim and sort of prickly. They pulled into the parking lot of The Tonk and he hopped out, heading around to her door to open it.

"What is it with the men in this town and these damned trucks? Can't you all have cars that aren't fifty feet off the ground?"

He helped her get down and tried not to smile. "You're just a bitty thing, I'll have to get a ladder for your side. Not that I don't like helping you in and out but..."

"My God you talk a lot."

He looked at her, surprised but her grin brought a matching one back to his lips. "You're kinda spunky for someone so small."

She took his arm and *hmpf*ed.

Tate was nervous as hell. She'd never been to The Tonk but was thankful that through the sea of people she sighted her sisters and brother across the room. They appeared to be sitting with a bunch of Chases. God, they all looked so pretty. There she was, a dumpling in a dress and everyone else was pretty. Figured.

Still, the music caught her within moments. The way it always did. And she didn't feel so much like a dumpling anymore. She felt graceful and a little bit sexy.

"Looks like you're a girl who loves to dance. Which is lucky for me, 'cause I'm a guy who loves girls who love to dance. Fate is a beautiful thing." He spun her into his arms and swayed a bit. "I like the way you feel against me."

"My word you're quite the flatterer." So much so it made her all giddy and weak-kneed. "I love to dance. Always have. We go to Reba's every other Saturday."

He kissed her and spun her again, leading her through the crowd toward the other side of the club where their family awaited. Only the disbelieving stares directed toward them made Tate uncomfortable and pissed off.

"Hi, honey, you look beautiful." Nathan stood to kiss Tate's cheeks, sensing her distress.

"Thank you. You all look fetching as well." She grinned at her sisters and Anne's boyfriend Royal before turning to the Chases assembled there. "Hi, everyone."

"I think you know most everyone. Kyle and Maggie, Liv and Marc were at my place a couple of weeks back. The big lunk there is my oldest brother Shane, his wife Cassie. Guys, this is Tate." Matt pulled a chair out for her and she sat down, feeling very grateful for her family there.

"Nice to meet those of you I haven't met before. While we're introducing folks, this is my brother Nathan, he teaches at the high school with Maggie. My sisters Beth and Anne and Anne's boyfriend Royal Watson."

"We've all introduced ourselves but we hadn't met Matt yet." Nathan squeezed her hand briefly.

"Tate and I have an appointment with the dance floor. When our waitress comes by can you order me a beer? Tate, sweetness, what would you like?"

"Oh, beer is fine."

Matt stood and escorted her through the crowd down to the

dance floor just as the music changed to something slow. He pulled her close against his body and eased her into the dance. Right off they matched. Their rhythm was the same, and everything else but the music and his pale green eyes on her fell away. She studied his face in the low light. He was the kind of handsome that was nearly pretty but not quite. His nose was just a little bit crooked but it's what took him straight into masculine handsome. High cheekbones defined his face and a light beard covered his chin and edged the line of his jaw. All in all, it made everything inside her go gooey.

Dangerous to let him make her feel that way but she couldn't seem to grasp her caution with him so close. Swaying there, their bodies moving as one she might almost believe he could love her. And even if he didn't, it didn't matter. He treated her with respect, made her feel sexy and funny, there was simply no reason she could see to not enjoy him.

"You're so beautiful, Tate. Have I told you that lately?" he murmured, dipping his head to kiss her temple and then her lips.

But *that* bugged her. It was like he said it just to say it or something. Beautiful was Cassie Chase or Liv. He'd run through his share of beautiful in his lifetime and his flattery, comparing her to them just made her mad.

"I don't need that stuff."

"What stuff? And why are you so pissy?"

"Pissy?"

"Yeah, you're cute with your chin jutted out and all but I like it when you're snuggled up to me even better."

"Look, I don't need compliments. Other women you're with may expect it, but I'm not them. I don't want empty flattery."

He stopped and pulled her out onto the back deck, past their families. Once outside she yanked her arm away from him and took a step back. "Don't ever manhandle me again."

Matt felt like she'd punched him in the stomach. What a fool he'd been. "I'm sorry. I didn't mean to make you feel unsafe with me. I just wanted to talk to you out here."

"Just ask me. I'm not a pet. Don't just yank me around like I've got no will of my own."

He couldn't help but be charmed, touched and really turned-on by the spark in her eyes.

"Of course. I didn't think."

She relaxed and he did as well.

"Now, repeat this bullshit about empty flattery, please. Because it sounded to me like you called me shallow."

"What? I'd never say that." She reached out and touched his cheek and he saw the sadness in her eyes. "I'm sorry. Did I make you feel that way?"

"We're both kinda touchy, huh?" He grinned. "Yeah, I felt that way. Why are you upset that I complimented you?"

"Look, I don't need that, okay? I'm all right that I'm not all supermodel gorgeous. I have eyes. You have eyes. I'm not Liv, I can't even knock on the door of the kind of beauty your brothers' wives have. Don't shit me because it insults me. We're here, I'm fine. I'm not some bimbo who needs to be massaged. You're totally in, right? You know you're getting some, so spare me the lubrication with the flattery."

Did she not know? He backed her against the railing and caged her with his arms. "Yes, my sisters-in-law are lovely women. But there's more than one kind of beautiful and none of them can hold a candle to you. You *are* beautiful. I'm not making that up. Although, it's nice to know I'm in later." He chuckled. "Tate, when I look at you, I see a beautiful woman. Curves in the right places, beautiful eyes, lips that call to me, your smile melts me. I don't say things I don't mean. Especially not to someone I care about and respect."

Because he couldn't resist, he leaned down and kissed her. It started slow but built until he was on fire for her.

"Well, now. Did you hit your head or can a real woman get in on this action?"

Stunned, Matt broke the kiss and looked up to see Melanie standing there, wearing a smirk.

"Slumming on the wrong side of town, Matt? Trust me, I'm better than she is in bed and my dad isn't an alkie and my mom's not a slut."

Not quite comprehending that anyone could be so cruel, Matt stepped in front of Tate to shield her from Melanie's verbal assault. But he should have known she wouldn't take being shielded that way. She stepped around him.

"Opposed to slumming on your side of town, Melanie? My goodness, is this what they're growing here on the pretty side of town these days? Hmm, big mouth, I can see the appeal. Too bad her brain's so small."

Matt put his arm around Tate's shoulder and saw her brother come out onto the deck.

"Everything all right out here?" Nate's face was guarded and Matt got the feeling this sort of thing wasn't unusual for them. It made the nausea he felt even worse.

"Just throwing out the trash. God, Nate, how is it you can stand being related to this fat bitch? You lucked out, you're not like the rest of them. Why do you associate with this scum?" Melanie turned to speak to Nathan.

Nathan blinked several times and Matt gasped. Tate was the only one who seemed unsurprised.

"Just when I think people can't get any worse, you go and

lower the bar, Melanie." Nathan shook his head as he moved toward Tate. But Matt was going to protect Tate, not anyone else.

"We all have our crosses to bear. Matt, I'd like to go." Tate's voice was remote, flat and it sent a chill down his spine.

"We're not going anywhere. You and I are here to dance. Nate, I think you and I need to share a beer when your sister and I are done dancing." Matt guided Tate back into The Tonk, keeping his body between her and Melanie at all times.

Melanie grabbed his arm. "Remember what you come from, Matt Chase. She's a fat nobody, you come from better. *We* come from better."

He shook himself free with a sneer. "You could have fooled me, Melanie. You best be aware that Tate's my girlfriend, I won't tolerate any nonsense." He continued past her and back toward their table.

He felt sick and saw Maggie watching Melanie with narrowed eyes. Cassie leaned in and spoke to Beth, appearing to hold her back. Anne had a look on her face that scared the hell out of him but luckily she stayed seated. Liv whispered in Maggie's ear and he worried all hell would break loose any moment. Not that Melanie deserved to be spared the wrath of every angry person at the table, but he didn't want Tate to feel any worse than she already did.

"What just happened?" Beth demanded and Tate shook her head. Nathan told them and gasps sounded around the table.

"I can't believe that bitch!" Maggie hissed.

"Oh I'm gonna smack a bitch down," Anne growled but Tate reached out and touched her sister's arm.

"Please don't do this. I don't want to make a big deal out of it." Matt hated that she sounded so resigned to the treatment she'd just received.

"Tate, when I first came here with Kyle you should have seen the way some of them reacted. I know how it feels. We're on your side. People like her aren't the majority and even if they were, they don't count." Maggie shook her head vehemently as she spoke.

"Tate I'm sorry you had to be subjected to that kind of thing. Melanie is—" But Tate interrupted Matt before he could finish.

"Just saying what half the women in here are thinking. I really don't feel well and I'd like to go. I can catch a ride with Beth if you want to stay here." Tate wouldn't meet his eyes.

He took her shoulders gently. "Don't you go away on me. I don't give a crap what anyone else thinks but my family and you. You got me? You don't let these small-minded idiots chase you off. Please, stay here with me. Let's dance."

"Tate, don't let the Melanies of the world ruin this. Matt is here with you. She's jealous. Show her you're better than she is," Beth said softly.

"Listen to your sister, sweetness." Matt kissed her.

Tate sighed. "Okay, okay. Let's get dancing then."

Relieved, he stood and helped her up before leading her to the dance floor.

She was graceful and sexy as she moved. He'd never seen a more natural dancer than Tate Murphy. He loved the way she lost herself in the music.

After another couple of hours he leaned over and whispered in her ear, "Sweetness, I'm dead on my feet. Do I still have that in? Because I have condoms and after a cup of coffee, I'll be ready for you."

She threw back her head and laughed and that simple thing filled him with joy.

"Let's go then. I have condoms too."

They said their goodnights and headed out into the evening. He didn't fail to notice the sneers and outright hostility some of the people showed toward Tate as they left.

"If we go to your place do you think I could squeeze breakfast out of you in the morning? You're a damn fine cook as well as being mighty lovely to look at."

"I've never met a man more full of it." Tate shook her head but could only barely stifle a smile.

"Does that mean yes?"

"I suppose so. You don't have to sleep over you know. I wouldn't be insulted if you wanted to go."

"Tate, you don't know me all that well so I'll excuse you this one last time. I'm gonna repeat, I don't say things I don't mean. I wouldn't have angled for breakfast if I hadn't wanted to stay over."

She drew a breath and nodded. "All right."

"That's my girl." He pulled into her driveway and escorted her to the door. She bustled around, kicking off her shoes before padding into her kitchen.

"I'm starting a pot of coffee," she called out and he wandered in, smiling at her.

"You look good with your shoes off. I like it. I like being here. Your house is nice, comfortable."

She smiled. "Thank you. I wanted to build a home. I..." She trailed off, turning quickly to open the cabinet and pull down two mugs.

"You what?"

"Do you take sugar?"

He put his hand out to stop her movement. "You what? Tell me. Share with me."

"I didn't grow up in a home. I grew up in a place where I slept. Sometimes. A lot of the time I didn't sleep because I wanted to be sure my brothers and sisters were okay. I saw this place and I knew I wanted it. I knew I could make it into a place where I could sleep safely. Where my siblings could come and feel safe too. God, Matt, you should go. We are so different it's not funny."

His stomach clenched. "Tate, why would I leave? We aren't that different. Not really. We both think family is important. We're close to the people we love. We're so much alike."

"Tell me, what's your memory of your eighth birthday?"

He smiled. "My dad took me and my brothers out to the lake. We went camping and I caught this piddly little catfish. He skinned it and cooked it up like it was the biggest fish ever caught. He tells people about it to this day. You'll like my dad, he's a good man."

"I bet he is. You know what my eighth birthday was like?"

He shook his head warily.

"My mother left the night before my birthday. Beth was a year old, so tiny. But I was already more of a mother to her than ours was. My father went on a bender after he beat the hell out of Tim for protecting me from the intended beating. I had to stay home from school on and off for two weeks to take care of Beth, Nathan and William, none of them were in school yet. Tim and I traded off going to school back and forth to keep the welfare workers away."

Matt swallowed hard. He couldn't imagine.

She put her hands in front of her face a moment and then pointed at him angrily. "Don't. God, don't look at me with pity in your eyes. I didn't tell you that for pity, I told you to underline the differences between us, Matt. Other kids had it worse. At least I had a bed to sleep in. I have a good life now. I own a business, a home. I don't need pity."

He looked down at her, small, her hands fisted at her sides. Damn, when did he start feeling so protective of her? Need welled up then as he reached out slowly to cup her cheek.

"I don't pity you." He bent to kiss her but when she was barefoot, he had to bend his knees to reach her. Instead, he picked her up and sat her on her kitchen counter, making a space between her thighs to get to her. "Give me your mouth, sweetness. I need that."

Tate didn't quite know how to handle it when he did that. He heard the bad stuff and still wanted her. Not out of pity. It unnerved her. And yet, she still wanted the hell out of him. Giving in to her desire, she reached up, sifting her hands through his hair and fisted, grabbing him and pulling him to her.

His kiss was eager and passionate. A moan of approval came from him as his hand swept up her neck to cradle her head while he continued his sensual assault on her lips.

He broke away long enough to speak against her mouth. "You taste good enough to eat, Tate. I think I need a snack to tide me over," he murmured as he moved up to nibble on her ear lobe. Tate gasped as he ran his tongue around the outer edge and dipped it inside.

Waves of warmth headed down her neck, over her nipples, straight to her pussy. She melted, molding her body to his.

The coffeemaker beeped that it was done and he sighed softly, stepping back and helping her down off the counter.

"Let's take that into the bedroom, shall we? We can sip between smooches."

Blinking quickly, she gulped and poured two big mugs, adding sugar whether he liked it that way or not.

She took both mugs and led the way down the hall to her bedroom. He watched as she placed them on the small table in the corner and turned shyly.

She laughed. "You sure you don't want to run away?"

He got serious and shook his head. "I don't want anything but to be inside you, Tate Murphy." He paused. "You don't have any idea what you do to me do you?"

"I don't understand it. Why me?"

Remaining there in the doorway, he knew she was nervous. She picked up the mug of coffee she'd just put down and took a sip. He didn't fail to notice the slight tremble of her hands as she did.

"Sweetness, I want you so much I think I'm going to have a stroke. All the blood in my body is now in one spot and I'm slightly dizzy from it," he said with a rueful grin as he motioned toward his cock. "Can I show you how much I want you? What you do to me? Again? Because if you recall, we were in a similar situation last weekend. Only now we've got condoms."

She nodded, staying silent. He took one step and then another and another until he reached her. He switched on the light and took a sip of the coffee. "Ahh, nice and sweet like a proper Southern woman knows how to make it." He winked.

She smiled, shaking her head at him.

"I want to see you," he said, coming to stand in front of her. Finishing the last of the coffee, he got down to business, popping buttons on her dress one by one.

"Turn off the light," she whispered.

"No, I won't be able to see you if I do that. I want to see your curves, sweetness. We did it your way last time. Let me see you."

"But..." She blushed and he paused to quickly pull his own

shirt off, tossing it in the nearby chair.

"See, I'll go first."

"Yeah, like that's a comparison," she grumbled but he couldn't help but love the way she stared at his body. It wasn't that he hadn't been sized up by the fairer sex before. But this was different, this was Tate looking at him like he was the best thing since Christmas morning.

"Sweet holy fuck. Oops, sorry, my fuck problem again. You're beautiful. Matt..." she hesitated, wringing her hands, "...I'm not...my body isn't like yours."

He chuckled and kissed her quickly. "I should hope not. Not that there's anything wrong with that." With a grin, he took her hand and put it over his cock. "This is what your body does to me. I'm not lying when I say you're sexy."

He got back to work until the last button on her dress slid free. Slowly, gently, he slid the dress back, letting it drop. She stood there for a moment, blushing, her eyes screwed shut tight.

Reaching out, he drew a fingertip down the curve between her breasts, right along the lace of the sexiest red lace bra he'd ever seen. Her panties matched, high cut on her hips. She was a little Venus there, delicate and yet larger than life.

"You still with me, sweetness? You're so damned beautiful, so sexy. I can't believe you wanted to hide yourself in the dark. Your skin is amazing, flawless." He smoothed his palms over her arms, down her stomach and around to cup her ass briefly.

Her eyes opened a little bit but she still looked dubious. He'd have to change that. Tracing the lace of her bra, he reached around and undid the hooks, letting it fall and join the dress.

Such pretty, alabaster-pale skin. He saw the faint tracery of blue veins just beneath. Her breasts were large and heavy in his hands, nipples hard and dark pink. They hardened further when he brushed his thumbs across them. He looked up to see her catch her lip between her teeth. Still, nervousness vibrated through her and he could tell by the way she stood she wanted to cover up.

Murmuring softly, he lay her down on the bed and eased her panties off. A triangle of closely trimmed pale curls shielded her pussy. She moved her hands to cover herself but he took them, kissing each one and putting them down on the bed.

"Please don't try and hide yourself. You are so damned beautiful and sexy I can't wait to be inside of you," he growled, pulling off his pants and shorts.

Her eyes widened as he stalked toward her and he was pleased by the look of hunger on her face.

He got to the bed next to her and she smiled up at him. "Now, where was I?" He waggled his brows.

Taking a deep breath, Tate sat up on her heels. "You'll have to wait," she said and took his cock into her hands. He slid his palms up her arms and into her hair but when she took him into her mouth, his head lolled back.

"Ahhh, you're so sweet. Heaven on Earth," he murmured, caressing her scalp. Her hands stroked the length of his cock when it wasn't in her mouth, palmed his sac, ran over the muscles of his thighs and dug into the flesh there with her nails, pulling him closer to her, deeper.

He watched as that pale, sunny hair slid forward, hiding her and revealing her in turns. She may have been shy but she certainly wasn't shy about making him feel good. He loved that. They were far more evenly matched in bed than he'd first imagined they'd be and the surprise was a good one. He knew from the weekend before that she was tireless and inventive and tonight was no different.

And yet it was. He felt like it was the very real beginning of everything he wanted to have with her for the future. She'd let him in just a bit. Told him some about her childhood and she was there, naked with the lights on. That trust in him was as much an aphrodisiac as anything ever had been.

He'd wanted her too much in the last days to hold out very long. When orgasm hit, he groaned and shuddered, her name a sigh on his lips.

Moments later, she moved away from him and he settled in, bringing her body close to his. "Give me a few years and I'll be right with you," he mumbled into her hair and she laughed softly.

Stroking the velvet skin at her hip, he marveled at how she felt. Coming back to himself, he kissed her face, her lips, her jaw and down the line of throat. He tasted her thundering pulsebeat as he moved down her chest and kissed over the curve of one breast. When he sucked a nipple into his mouth she sobbed out a gasp.

"Responsive, perfect. You're perfect," he said with approval and he raked his teeth across the sensitive tip and she shuddered. He rolled the other nipple between his fingers and she writhed beneath him. He slid his hand down her stomach and through her curls and found her hot and wet as he stroked her.

She smelled sweet and spicy and the heat of her skin drove him wild. He kissed down her chest, rimming her belly button with his tongue.

"Hmm, I've been here before. I like it." Scooting down, he settled between her thighs, putting them on his shoulders. She sobbed out again, arching off the bed when he dipped his mouth to her sex.

Tate was sure she'd never in her life felt more desired, more desirable. He ate her up with his gaze, with his hands and his mouth. He took the time to learn her, find what made her tick, what made her writhe and beg.

There with him in her bed, with the pale light of her bedside lamp on her nakedness, she felt all right. He didn't look at her with distaste, he looked at her with longing. She knew she wasn't comparable to Liv, but at the same time he desired her and that made things all right.

With his mouth on her pussy, he pushed and pushed her toward coming. With him it was easy, she'd been halfway there just smelling his cologne as they danced at The Tonk. But his very talented fingers and tongue devastated her.

A nearly feral groan came from deep in her throat as she shuddered. He hummed his approval, sending the vibrations up through her clit. He lapped at her and learned all of the things that drove her wild and finally, after making her beg for it, pushed her over and made her come.

"Don't go anywhere," he whispered as he leaned over and rustled through his pants, holding up a condom with a triumphant smile.

"Even if my legs worked I wouldn't leave my bed with you there."

Cocking his head, he looked at her, his smile softening.

"So you gonna moon at me all night or get with the condom application so you can do me?"

Startled a moment, he laughed and ripped the packet open to quickly roll the condom on.

"You know, you look like butter wouldn't melt and then you open your mouth. There's a smartass living inside you, Tate. I like that. A sex goddess and a smartass."

He said it as he moved back between her thighs, which she

happily widened to admit him. He probed her entrance, teasing her with the head of his cock but she wrapped her legs around him and grabbed his ass. She needed him, it'd been a very long, very frustrated week. Surging her hips up and pulling him toward her with a handful of his ass, she brought him into her with one hard thrust.

She felt the intrusion of his cock straight up her spine. She'd never felt so full before. It wasn't like he had a king-sized penis, it was good, did the job quite nicely. But it was made for her.

Suddenly, she felt a lot more exposed than just being naked with the lights on. She pushed it all away, all the emotions that weren't just about how good he felt. There'd be time for panic later on.

"Jesus!" he gasped out. She was scalding hot and really tight. It'd been a while for her or she did those exercises to make her pussy tight. He doubted those worked this well though.

Trying to concentrate and not come two minutes after he got inside her body, he stopped moving. Instead, he leaned down and flicked his tongue over one nipple and then the other, alternating as he felt like it. She made tiny, gaspy, needy sounds that eroded his control even more.

He began to slowly move inside of her, sliding almost all of the way out and then inexorably back in again. She met him thrust for thrust, his hands at her hips, tracing the curves there, her strong legs holding him to her—*as if there was another place on earth she'd rather have been.*

So this was making love. This was the intensity of connection with the person you cared about more than anything else. "Tate, I..." He broke off, it was a bad idea to tell someone you loved them during sex wasn't it? "I feel so good, *you* feel so good."

He teased her with short, shallow, slow digs of his cock, delighting in how she writhed and tried to get more from him. He loved teasing her, drawing out her pleasure and being the one to deliver it to her.

She tightened her inner muscles around him, making him gasp.

"Oh man, that felt good," he said with a groan.

"I'll do it more if you just let me come," she panted out, doing it again, causing his balls to nearly crawl back into his body.

"Deal." He picked up his pace, moving a hand to where they were joined. Her hips jutted forward when he flicked a finger across her clit. He thrust and she tightened, he flicked and she rolled her hips until she bowed off the bed, a deep, earthy moan breaking from her.

Her pussy clutched at him, pulling at his body as if she couldn't bear to let him go. He tried to ride it out but she pulled him under. He pulsed as she did, his head back, muscles taut.

He fell to the side and they both lay there panting for a few moments. He got up briefly and came back to her. She'd gotten under the sheets and he joined her, snuggling against her body.

ॐ

Long after she'd felt him drift off into sleep, Tate lay awake, listening to the tick of the hallway clock as the minutes slid past.

She'd moved past panic and into terror and back to unease with her feelings about Matt Chase.

She wasn't a virgin. She wasn't super experienced or

anything but she'd been with several men and had good times in bed with almost all of them.

But what she'd experienced with Matt Chase that night was more than a good time. What she'd experienced was a huge leaping sprawl into holy-fuck-I-may-love-this-guy territory.

And she could not love Matt Chase. She was a Murphy. He was a Chase. Buildings in the town were named after his family! He was beautiful and charming and came from an ease and privilege that she'd have resented a few years before. Still made her uncomfortable. He was a man who never had to fear being hungry or being hurt by someone he loved and was supposed to be protected by. She'd lay odds he'd never seen either one of his parents drunkenly angry.

There was a whole universe between her world and his and she'd never fit in. He'd come to see that in time and he'd find some suave way of dumping her and she'd go back to her side of the street and he to his.

She could not love Matt Chase and she couldn't let him make it happen either.

Chapter Seven

The next morning they'd had a nice breakfast but Matt could tell she was holding herself back from him and he didn't like it one bit. And he had no plans to let her get away with it either.

"So I sort of told my mother you're coming to dinner at their house tonight." He sipped his coffee and sopped up the gravy on his plate with a biscuit. She was the best cook he'd never met, even better than his mother. If the woman hadn't been everything he'd ever wanted otherwise, he'd still have wanted to keep her for her skills in the kitchen.

She jerked her head back and put her fork down. She'd eaten fruit and just one biscuit, much to his consternation.

"What? Why would you have done such a thing? I'm having dinner with my family here tonight. We do every other Sunday."

"My momma's gonna be so disappointed."

"Matt, I'm sorry but I have plans with my family."

"Can't you break them just this once? Have dinner with them tomorrow night? My parents are expecting you and you know my mother, she'd take it awful hard if you didn't come."

Her eyes widened and he knew he'd gone too far.

"In the first place, I would *never* ask you to dump off a family commitment for me. In the second place, I would never dump a family commitment for something like a sneak dinner invitation that you didn't even bother asking me for. I have nieces and a nephew, they have school during the week so I wouldn't interrupt their weeknight schedule just to suit your whim. In the third place, my family is very important to me and I don't appreciate you treating it otherwise. Lastly, don't you ever try and guilt me with your mother like that."

Knowing he'd been rightfully busted he put his coffee down and reached out to take her hands. "I'm sorry. You're right, I shouldn't have asked you to choose like that. It wasn't fair. Next Sunday will you come to dinner at my parents' house? Assuming you don't do dinner with your family in those off Sunday nights?"

"I don't know, Matt. This is moving so fast. I..."

"Fast? We've known each other for a few months, that's not fast. Come on, Tate, look, let me just go ahead and put it all on the line and be totally straight with you. I really like you. I enjoy your company and I want to be with you. I want us to continue dating and I want to see where this can go. This is not a casual thing for me. I'm old enough to know what I want and you're it, Tate Murphy."

"You can't know what you're saying." She pushed back from the table and began to pace. The silky red shortie robe she wore fluttered around as she moved.

So on the ropes, his little Venus. He grinned. He knew then what had to happen. He'd helped every single one of his brothers with the wooing of their future wives so he had enough experience. Clearly Tate was caught up in their supposed differences again and he'd have to drag her, kicking and screaming, hopefully in the throes of orgasm, into love with him.

He leaned back in his chair and watched her. "I know

exactly what I'm saying, Tate. I'm well on my way to being in love with you."

She spun, sputtering. He had to bite his cheek to keep from laughing.

"Love? Fuckadoodledoo! You've had sex before last night, right? I've heard enough stories about your prowess to know you have. I promise to let you in my bed again, you don't have to tell me you love me to get back in."

"Little Venus, gorgeous, I know I don't have to tell you I love you to get back between those silky, pale thighs of yours." His voice lowered and he winked at her, loving the way she blushed and fanned herself briefly. "But the truth is, I do love you." He shrugged.

"Matthew Chase! You can't love me! I'm a fat little nobody from a horrible family from the wrong side of the road. You're meant to be with a woman who knows how to use all the right forks, a woman who knows how to pick linens. A woman who has buildings named after her family."

He stood and moved to her, so angry he barely remembered moving. "You will not talk about yourself like that." He took her arms and kissed her hard. "You are someone. You're Tate Murphy. You work hard, you built your life from nothing and I couldn't possibly care less about forks or linens. You don't think much of me if you think I'd care about all that stuff more than what's inside a person."

"What's inside? Matt, you have no idea what kind of genes I'm carrying."

"You don't scare me, Tate. We're not the sum of our parents you know. You aren't. None of your siblings is from what I can tell. You're not his anyway, even if I was concerned. Isn't that what you told me?"

Her eyes widened and he raised a brow. "What, think you

can scare me away with rough talk? Not. Going. To. Happen."

"This is just crazy talk."

He nodded. "It is. Now will you come to dinner next Sunday and can I come over here tonight after I finish up at my parents'? I'm not going to let you push me away. The cooking's too good and you're hot in bed."

She shoved her hair back away from her face, frown lines etched into her forehead. "You don't love me, Matt. This can't be anything more than some fun evenings."

"Tate, don't tell me I can't love you. It's too late and it already is more than some fun evenings. If I didn't know you were so scared, I'd be offended and thinking you just wanted to use me for my great big penis."

She fought a smile and he realized the warmth in his chest was her, the way he felt about her. Love. He'd never felt it before but he knew he never wanted to be without it again. She made him whole.

"Your penis is just fine, Matt. But just what exactly do you envision this being?"

One arm banded around her waist, he pulled her back to the table and down into his lap. "Don't want this to get cold," he said, picking up the remains of his bacon. "Damn, you're a fine cook. What I foresee this being, Venus, is we date and date and have lots of sex and you get to know my family and I get to know yours and then I ask you to marry me and we get married and have a passel of kids and our house will always be full of busybody relatives."

She closed her eyes. "Marriage and kids? We've been on one date, two if you count that first time at the diner. That's not fast?"

"Every single lunch from May to now was a date."

"This can't happen. Look, let's just date, have fun. Leave the marriage talk out of the equation."

"Are you saying I'm only good enough to fuck?"

"Just go. Get your stuff and go." But she said it with no conviction at all and he waved it off.

"I'm not going anywhere, Tate Murphy. Not in the way you're suggesting. You need to know that right now. I don't give up when there's something worthy of working for. You may think I'm some soft, shallow guy who doesn't know what it means to struggle and maybe that's true in a lot of ways. But damn it, I'm worthy of you."

"What the fuck are you talking about? This isn't about you! This is about me."

He stood, setting her on her feet gently before kissing her forehead. "I'm going to get going. Not because I'm going for good but I need to help Kyle do some work in my parents' yard this morning."

"I'm...I don't want to hurt your feelings, Matt. I don't think you're soft and shallow. God, I don't even know where you get that. You're wonderful and handsome and funny and sweet. And you're not for me. Can't you see that? Can't you see how wrong I am for you?"

"I'm not arguing with you over that point, Tate. It's a stupid fucking point and I'm not discussing it." He shrugged into his shirt and sat to lace his shoes. "I'll be here tonight after dinner with my parents. I hear you make excellent dessert."

"Matt, are you listening to me?"

He stood, pulling her to him and brought his mouth to hers and kissed the hell out of her. "Of course I am. But you're wrong. I'll see you later. And I'll be back between those thighs again too, Tate. Don't think you can hold yourself away from me. I want you, you want me. It's that simple."

He strode out the back door and she stood in the kitchen, the morning sun shining through the window as she heard him get into his truck and go.

"I am in big trouble."

&

Polly Chase watched Matt tear through his meal. *Good Lord, finally.* "You have someplace else to be?"

He sighed explosively and put his fork down. "Okay, Momma, I need your help."

She sat back and smiled at him and then at his father who chuckled. "Tate Murphy?"

"How'd you know?"

"Son, she's a witch. Didn't growing up with her as your momma teach you anything? You can't hide it from her." Edward amused himself entirely too much. Polly winked at him and frowned a moment. The scamp was utterly unrepentant and winked back, taking her hand and kissing it. She married him for a reason and she'd collect her payback after everyone left.

"Matthew, you asked me about her. I've seen you in town with her a few times. I heard you took her to The Tonk last night." She laughed, seeing his surprise. "Honey, who do you think the gossip about the last single Chase boy comes to first? I know you eat lunch with her three times or more a week. I know you ate dinner with her last Sunday night at The Sands. I know you slept at her place last night too." She raised an eyebrow at him. "I've just been waiting for you to ask me. I take it she's holding herself back? Telling you she's not right for a Chase?"

Maggie looked up and Polly laughed again. Young people! All one needed to do was keep their eyes open and their ears ready. People weren't that hard to read.

"Yes. Stupid isn't it? I told her I loved her this morning and she told me she just wanted to have a good time."

"What? She thinks she's better than you? I say you're better off without her then!" Liv snorted.

Polly hid a smile. Liv was a smart girl.

"No! She just said it to blow smoke. Stupid woman said a bunch of stuff about linens and forks and me needing to be with a woman with buildings named after her family. She thinks she's, and this is her words, *a fat nobody from the wrong side of the road.*"

Liv winked at Polly before turning back to Matt. "And you said?"

"I told her she *was* someone and not to talk about herself like that. I also said I didn't care about any of that shit. Uh, stuff, sorry, Momma. I want to marry her."

"Wow, that was fast." Shane put his napkin down and looked at Matt. "You sure?"

"I've been sure since I watched her building block towers with Nicholas last month. I know it here." He pressed the heel of his hand over his chest. "I'm old enough to know the difference between liking a woman and loving one. I sure as heck haven't ever loved one before."

Polly shrugged with a grin. "Well then, we'll bring her into the fold won't we? And her brothers and sisters too. You know you won't just be getting a wife right?"

"That's what I love so much about her, Momma. All the women I've been with haven't ever thought about family the way I have." He quickly looked at Liv. "Well, Liv but that was different. Anyway, she has such a love and commitment to them and they to her. So protective of her. You should have seen them at The Tonk when Melanie said a bunch of stuff about her. I thought we were going to have to hold her sister Beth back from taking Melanie out."

Polly's smile was nearly feral. Matt wanted Tate and so that made Tate hers too. Anyone who meant harm to the girl or her family would have to deal with the consequences and that meant Polly.

"I heard about Melanie." Polly waved it away. "She'll need a talking to. But, cookie, you know you're going to have to deal with a lot of the same, right? Tate *does* come from the bad side of town. Her parents are awful people and she's not as comely as the other women you've dated. Not that she isn't beautiful, don't you give me that look, Matthew. But I didn't raise you to pretend the obvious doesn't exist and if you don't confront it, it'll hurt her. Love isn't about a dress size, neither is beauty and it certainly isn't about a bank account. But it's gonna be said so we have to be ready for it.

"Each one of my daughters came to me in her own special package but one thing they all have in common is that they're stunning women. Without even knowing them, you look at them and they make your heart beat faster. Maggie had to deal with some jealousy issues but frankly, Tate will have it the hardest. You're going to have to be very up front and very vocal that Tate is your choice."

Matt nodded and Polly began to plan.

"Thanks, Momma."

"Of course, cookie. That's what family does. I take it you're eating your food at three times the normal speed to go to her? Why didn't you invite her here?"

"I started to talk to you about it earlier this week but I got busy with work. I invited her this morning but I sort of tried to guilt her into it." He told her of what he'd done that morning and Tate's reaction.

"Matthew, I'm appalled. I am happy to see the girl put you in your place after that. Things have come very, very easy for you. Too easy I think. You've never had to struggle. Always top marks in school, top of your class at the academy, you've always excelled at whatever you put your mind to. And never had to break a sweat to do it. Now you boys know I love you all equally but Matt, you're the handsomest one of the crew. You grin and flutter your lashes and the girls have always bent into pretzels to please you. This one is skittish, you need to be blunt and up front with her at all times. Yes, be charming and handsome, it's who you are, but don't rely on that to do the work. *You* do the work."

"I thought I was the handsomest," Shane grumbled.

"Shane, you're the biggest and bravest. Kyle is the kindest and most compassionate. Marc? He's the sweetheart charmer. All of you are handsome, you know that so don't try and play me. But Matthew here? Ahh, he's nearly pretty he's so handsome. Smart too, but handsome has done the work for him. He's just realizing that now and he's feeling a bit bad about it. Don't feel bad, cookie. You're a good man, a lot better than you give yourself credit for. You've found your special girl, that's everything. You'll build a life with her and she'll be part of us and you'll be part of her kin. Our family will get larger by eight, or fourteen because there are wives and children. Ahh, more grandchildren for me." She smiled.

Matt wanted to put his head in her lap. No one understood him better than she did. He shouldn't have waited so long. It felt so *good* that she knew him so well. He looked around the table at the family he loved and who had his back. Damned lucky.

101

"Go on. Tell her she's invited here next week. Invite them all. I hear she's a good cook. That so?"

Matt nearly choked on his tea, he wasn't going there. "Sure. I won't go hungry."

"Better baker than Maggie?"

"Okay on that note, I'm going to get going. Thank you for the support." He got up and kissed his mother's cheek while his father chuckled.

"I'll walk you out."

His father walked to the door with him. "Nice one. She's really better than Maggie or your momma?"

"Daddy, I've never eaten biscuits that I'd have sold my soul for until this morning. And she made them while she did three other things."

Edward laughed again. "Look, Matt, her daddy, I didn't want to say anything in front of the others, Shane may know it though, being sheriff and all. Her daddy is a thug and a violent one. Keep an eye out. He's a wastrel too. I wouldn't be surprised if he hit you up for cash. Watch yourself. And her too, it can't be easy on her coming from that when she's such a good person."

"It isn't, I can tell. But the rest of them are good people."

"Course they are. You wouldn't have loved her elsewise. Don't rush up on the girl. Let her know how you feel but she's a person who's been abandoned and disappointed and lied to by people she should have been able to trust. It's gonna be a bit like she's a wounded animal, I know that's not entirely an accurate comparison but it's close enough for you to know what I mean."

Matt's father didn't hand out advice right and left. He knew people better than most because he listened more than he spoke. Kyle was a lot like him, Matt realized.

"It's hard. I want to scoop her up and protect her."

Edward smiled and squeezed his son's shoulder. "I know. That's why you know this is real, the fear of losing it or her."

"You're pretty smart for an old guy."

"Smartass. Now get on out of here. If you promised her you'd stop in, do it. Keep your promises to her, no matter what."

"Thanks, Daddy."

"That's what I'm here for, boy."

߂

"Why don't you call him?" Nathan asked her softly as she looked to the front door for the hundredth time.

"I don't know what you're...oh fuck me, he said he'd stop in after dinner. It's not like it's a date. He probably just forgot. It's not a big deal." Tate knew it was useless to try and lie to Nathan.

The house had been loud and chaotic and filled to the rafters with Murphys but now with bellies filled and coffee making to go with the cherry pie she'd baked earlier that day, things had quieted down. The kids played out back in the twilight.

"Tate, if the man made a promise, he's meant to keep it. If he doesn't, he's not worth caring about."

Tate put her head on Nathan's shoulder a moment before Tim noticed. If Tim saw her in any distress at all he'd go into protective mode right away. So far that evening he'd been on kid duty so she'd been spared his usual close monitoring of her moods.

She moved into the kitchen when the coffeemaker beeped. Beth followed along with Anne to slice pie and get coffee for everyone. Tim came in to get milk and pie for the kids.

Tate smiled, her life was good. When she was Belle's age she'd never have imagined her life would be so wonderful as an adult. Matt Chase or not.

But when she made her way back into the dining room with a tray of plates with pie, she caught sight of the man she'd been trying so hard not to think of come in through her front door.

He grinned as he caught sight of her. "I see I got here just in time. Do I smell cherry pie?"

She smiled back before she could even think about it. "There's enough for you most likely. Have a seat there." She indicated a chair with a tilt of her chin and he rolled his eyes, approaching to take the tray from her and place it on the table.

"Thank you."

"I don't suppose I need to even ask if this is scratch pie."

Nathan snorted and grabbed a plate and a mug of coffee. "Better grab a slice now, there won't be a flake of that crust left over in about three minutes."

Matt sat and she smirked, pushing a plate to him following that with a mug of coffee. "It's decaf."

The kids came screaming into the house but got quiet when they caught sight of Matt sitting at the table. Tim gave her a subtle eyebrow raise and Susan chuckled quietly.

"This is Danny. Danny, this is Matt Chase." Her nephew took a bowl of ice cream and pie and sat at the small table kitty corner to the larger one. He eyed Matt carefully, making sure the stranger wasn't going to snatch his pie. Nodding his head in a very fine imitation of his father, he got down to eating.

Matt nodded solemnly, eating his own pie.

"And this is Shaye." Three-year-old Shaye waltzed into the room wearing a tutu and clutching her bowl.

"I don't like cherries. Tate made me peach pie 'cause I'm special. And you can't have none either."

Matt stifled his smile. "Pleased to meet you, Shaye. I promise not to steal your pie."

She re-introduced him to everyone else and explained that William and Cindy were home with their sick twins or there'd have been four more people there.

"Sit down, sweetness." Matt patted the chair next to where he sat and she did. He looked around the table and she knew what was coming next. "Hey, let me go and get you a slice of pie."

She put a hand on his arm to stay him. "No, I don't want any. I'm having coffee."

He narrowed his eyes at her and held a forkful of pie toward her mouth. "Take a bite of this pie and tell me why you aren't having a slice. Because I've never tasted better."

"Don't bother," Tim mumbled. "She won't."

"Don't interfere," his wife, Susan, murmured.

"He's right. Why we all sit here when she does this is beyond me. Tate, take a bite of the pie." Anne glared at her and Tate widened her eyes and then narrowed them, sending a non-verbal *back off* to her sister. One her sister ignored with a snort.

"Because *she* doesn't want any pie. Why are you all talking around me? I don't want any pie. It's not a national tragedy that Tate Murphy isn't having pie. Let it go." Shame and anger roiled in Tate's head. This wasn't something for outsiders. She hated it enough when it was just them but it didn't concern Matt and she didn't want him in the middle of her damned business. She'd have told them to shut up and fuck off but Danny and Shaye were there a few feet away and she didn't want them involved.

"Is this a regular thing? The not eating of pie?" Matt asked Tim.

"My father made us all messed up in our own special way." Her older brother looked at her totally unrepentant. Triumphant even that he'd gained another ally in his war against her refusal to eat dessert. It was stupid.

She crossed her arms over her chest and glared at them all. None of them seemed to care, which only made her angrier. It was her damned body, what she chose to do with it was her business. She didn't let her father control it and she wouldn't let anyone else either. If not eating pie pissed anyone else off, too bad. It had taken an awful lot of years to be okay with her shape and her size and she was! She didn't deny her own issues, she knew she had them, but they were hers and she'd deal with them in her own way.

Matt felt her tense up next to him. He glanced at her, noted the blush and looked at Tim. Relieved, he saw the concern on her older brother's face before remembering the moment in The Sands and her reaction to the pie there—her comment that she didn't eat dinner when she was around her father. His heart ached for the wounds she'd been dealt by her own damned father. Instead of railing about it, he sighed and thought about how he'd handle it.

"Tate took the brunt of it all for us. To protect us. He did the worst to her." Nate kept his eyes on his pie as he spoke and a chill worked its way down Matt's spine.

"Nathan, Tim, stop it now. You too, Anne. We don't need to relive it. *I* don't need to. All of you stop talking about me like I'm not here! While you're at it, remember the children are listening to everything we say."

"Well then, you talk to me." Lowering his voice, he turned to her, seeing her eyes spark but feeling enough spark of his own. He'd be damned if he let her asshole of a father abuse her when he wasn't even there.

"I don't want any fuh...freaking pie." She looked quickly at the children, who happily ate their pie and ice cream, before turning back to him. "That's all. I'm full. I had dinner and I sampled when I made it. It's not like I'm in any danger of wasting away." She made a frustrated motion at her body.

"And you're not in danger of exploding if you have a bite of this heaven on a fork either." Matt danced the fork in front of her but she was not amused.

"You need to stop this now, Matt," she told him softly and he reluctantly pulled the pie away but not before he saw the look of approval on her siblings' faces. Well, they liked him and were on his side in this thing.

"Fine. For now."

He finished as he visited with her family, getting to know them all, liking them tremendously. There was a great deal of familiarity there and he approved. They loved each other, made jokes and took care of each other. Tate would fit into his family just fine, and he would hers.

Everyone helped clean the kitchen and Matt didn't fail to notice Tate kept busy, avoiding being alone with him. Silly woman. She couldn't win when he wanted something. And he wanted her.

Tim and Susan left first with the kids and everyone else followed. Matt ignored her looks suggesting he go each time someone else left and he liked seeing her siblings ignore the hints too.

"Alone at last." He flopped back onto her couch, putting his feet up on her coffee table.

She bustled into the room and pushed his feet off with her bare one. "Get your feet off my table."

He grinned. "Sorry. Come sit here with me. I'm lonely and I've wanted to kiss you all night."

"Matt, I'm so tired."

He saw the edge of fear and panic on her face. She needed comfort and didn't want to need it. She broke his heart sometimes. God how he loved her.

Standing, he moved with purpose to where she stood and encircled her with his arms. "I know, sweetness. Let me. Let me ease it for you. Lean on me." He spoke, lips against the pale, cool silk of her hair.

"Why are you doing this?"

"I told you. I love you, Tate. Let me love you."

"You can't love me. You don't love me. You just feel sorry for me."

He sighed and walked her to her bedroom, turning off lights as he went.

"You talk too much about stuff you can't possibly know about. I know what I feel, Tate."

"I need to be alone, Matt."

"No you don't. You need to be held. I want you, yes. But tonight, let me hold you. I want to sleep with you against me. Will you let me stay here tonight?" He searched her face tenderly, loving the surprised and slightly confused flutter of her lashes.

"I don't know..."

"I do. Please, Tate." He'd never actually begged a woman to let him sleep in her bed, not even to fuck her, before. He needed her as much as he knew she needed him.

"All right. All right. I can't argue with you over it. I don't want to."

He smiled, leaning down to kiss her gently.

ℬ

Damn that Matthew Chase! Tate couldn't help but smile as she pushed her cart through the grocery store several days later. No matter how much she tried to push him away, he was there. Always there.

So thoughtful, too. She'd come home two nights before to find a new flower bed dug and planted. He and Kyle had spent part of their day doing it. All because she'd told him how she kept planning to do it but never had the time.

Reaching up, she touched the small silver Venus pendant he'd brought to her that morning at the shop. Said he'd seen it and it reminded him of her, wanted her to wear it against her skin and think of his lips there.

A shiver of delight headed up her spine.

All her delight evaporated as she turned the corner and saw Melanie standing there with Kendra Fosse and some other twit, Dolly somethingorother.

Melanie caught the cart as Tate attempted to steer around them.

"Go on then, say your piece and then move." Tate glared at Melanie.

"I shouldn't need to point out to you that you're in over your head, you gold digging whore."

The look on Melanie's face was pure hatred and Tate had

seen it more than once. She could never quite figure out why Melanie Deeds hated her so damned much. But they all treated the Murphy kids, especially Tate, badly. Because they could, she supposed. Where most of her siblings were tall and thin, her sisters were gorgeous and her brothers all hale and handsome, Tate was short, pale and fluffy. That made her otherness the biggest target.

"Excuse me? I take it this little scene is sour grapes because Matt and I are seeing each other?" Short, pale and fluffy or not, she wasn't about to take any guff from the likes of a snotty bitch like Melanie and her little cabal of mean girls. Mean girls way past thirty. She snickered.

"Seeing each other? Is that what you call it?"

"Get to the point, Melanie, the shrillness of your voice makes my teeth hurt and your fake tan is giving me a headache. Oh and do your roots for cripes' sake." Hee! That hit home. Melanie's pretty face crumpled on even more ire. Tate hoped she got a wrinkle Botox couldn't clear up.

"You keep your cheap, fat ass on your side of town. Matt Chase isn't meant for the likes of you."

Tate raised an eyebrow, a naturally blonde eyebrow. "Ahh, that's what this is about. Can't take it that he dumped you and came to me. Oh, that must sting that shriveled up, black heart of yours. All the money and good shoes in the world can't lure Matt from my bed to yours. I may be fat and cheap but I'm the one getting laid by Matt Chase. Guess you'll have to find some other guy because Matt is taken."

Melanie pushed the cart but Tate was stronger than she was and she pushed back, making Melanie step backward.

"Don't you push me, Melanie Deeds. You said your piece now get your ass out of the way or I'll run you over and smile while I do it."

"We'll see how funny you think this is when me and my friends boycott your ratty little salon."

Tate whipped her head around. "Oh no you did not just insult my salon! Look here, you stupid bimbo, you'd better have a salon visit somewhere in your future because your roots are so bad you look like you'd be at home next to my old trailer." She turned to Kendra who'd been smirking at Melanie's little tirade. "Although I'm sorry we can't help you. We don't do Botox."

"You slut! Just like your mother. You're not good enough to be a Chase, you just remember that. Matt Chase will get tired of you soon enough and you'll run back to your tacky little house and your cheap, buy-one-get-one free life with your cheap shoes and knock off bags. You're a nobody, Tate Murphy. A *fat* nobody who doesn't even know who her dad is." Melanie's face was red but Tate was the one who saw red.

"Get. Out. Of. My. Way." She shoved the cart menacingly and Melanie finally moved aside. "I'm Tate Murphy and I'm better than a thousand of you, Melanie Deeds. You know it too. If money bought worth, I'd still be better than you."

She blew past them and managed to finish her shopping instead of running out the doors in tears like they'd wanted her to.

Still, there'd been several cancellations for the rest of the week. It'd cost the shop several hundred dollars. But not her pride. Never, ever her pride.

Chapter Eight

Matt chuckled to himself as they approached his parents' front door. They were a sight to behold, Tate and Matt along with three of her siblings. His momma would be in hog heaven.

Add to it the bonus of having Tate be more comfortable because her family was with her for that first dinner at the Chase household. And it was a big night, they were celebrating Kyle's birthday, too. In another three weeks Nicholas would be a year old.

He remembered back to July of the year before, Maggie was heavy with pregnancy and Liv was just about to admit to herself that she loved Marc.

It'd hurt then. Just a bit. To see his brother finding love before he had, and with the woman Matt had been with a few years before that. But part of the hurt had been Matt's frustration that he just hadn't ever loved Liv, even though he'd wanted to. He'd wondered if he'd ever find what his brothers had found and here he was, his arm around the shoulder of the woman who made him whole.

Not that she made it easy. The woman was a pain in the ass. Skittish as hell. Defensive and so damned strong. He loved her so much and he knew she felt deeply about him too, figured it was love even. But she was scared and he couldn't do much more than ease her into life as his woman.

Thank God for her siblings who'd supported his relationship with her totally.

The door opened before he could reach the knob and his mother stood there, a great big grin on her face. Rushing onto the porch, she pulled Tate into a hug.

"Hey there, Tate. Don't you look pretty tonight?" Polly stood back and Matt realized his mother and Tate were roughly the same height. He stifled a laugh but looked up to see his father making the same discovery as he stood in the doorway.

Tate blushed. "Thank you so much for having us, Mrs. Chase. I know it's a family occasion and all. I told Matt we should come on a different night but he insisted."

Polly waved a hand at that. "Pshaw. Piffle even. Come on in. Hello, Anne and Beth, it's nice to see you two. And you're Nathan, right? We've met once at a town hall meeting about the new high school. Come on in!" She shooed everyone into the front hall.

Edward looked at Matt and then down at Tate, his face softening. Matt wanted to sigh with relief. His father would temper his mother's enthusiasm and make Tate feel at ease.

"Hello, darlin'. I'm Edward, Matt's daddy. Welcome to our home." Edward took her hand and kissed it and damned if Tate didn't actually emit a girlish giggle.

Edward winked at her and Polly snorted. "Edward, don't you go trying to trade me in on a younger model."

Edward shook his head at his wife, smiling. "My darling wife, I'd never trade you in. But I do hear Tate's quite the cook. I was just hedging my bets."

Tate laughed and Polly grinned at Matt.

Edward introduced himself to her siblings and put Tate's hand in the crook of his arm, escorting her into the family room where the other Chase boys and their assorted wives were already seated.

Tate saw Kyle and handed him a present, wishing him a happy birthday. Shane moved to her with purpose, giving her a kiss on the cheek and a hug as Cassie followed in his wake. Matt loved that his giant of a brother was so gentle with her. He supposed part of it was Cassie's doing.

Nicholas saw Tate, squealed in delight and toddled over. She knelt at his level and within moments lay on the carpet, driving cars around.

"My sister is a good person. Kind, smart. She'd do anything for the people she loves." Nathan stood with Matt as the rest of the group mixed and chatted.

"I love your sister, Nate."

"I know. She's afraid of it."

"Why? I'd never hurt her. She has to know that. I've never been violent or even angry with her. I'm always gentle." It tore him apart that she'd fear him.

Nathan sighed. "Matt, that's not it entirely. She's afraid to truly love you and have everything that makes the two of you so different come back to cause her pain. She's afraid that once you know all of it, everything about our parents, how we came up, you'll reject her."

"That's silly. I don't care about any of that stuff. Nate, I don't care where you grew up."

"You don't. But others do."

"Who cares about them?"

"She didn't tell you." Nathan hesitated and Matt tore his eyes away from Tate and Maggie playing on the floor with Nicholas to face her brother.

"Tell me what?"

"She's going to kill me. She needs to tell you herself."

"Fuck that. Come on, Nathan, you opened the subject up, just tell me." Matt kept his voice down, not wanting to alert her.

"Melanie and her friends cornered Tate at the market earlier this week. Taunted her. Said she was a gold digger. Called her a whore. They're boycotting the salon. She's lost some business."

Matt blinked, disbelief clouding his brain as he struggled to understand. "What? Why would they do that? Is there some old battle between them or something? I broke things off with Melanie two months before I walked into the salon for the first time and met Tate. I don't understand."

"Matt," Nathan shook his head, "you're a good guy but you don't know what it was like to grow up the way we did. Melanie has *always* been this way about our family. Well, mainly Tate. Always Tate because she's different. She..." He broke off, pressing his lips together.

"She what? Please, Nathan, she won't tell me any of this herself. I want to understand her, I want to protect her and I can't if I don't know."

"She's already going to be pissed I told you this much, Matt. She's ashamed. We all are but she's the worst. She protected us all at great risk to herself."

Sickness roiled through Matt's gut at the thought of her suffering. Of anyone hurting her, including Melanie. He'd have a few things to tell her when he ran her to ground.

"Dinner! Come on, everyone." Polly clapped her hands to get attention and Nicholas copied her.

Kyle laughed, scooping his son up and heading toward the dining room.

Matt went to Tate, holding his hand out to help her up, and

the smile she gave him as she took it melted any anger he'd had at her for not telling him right away.

Nathan cornered her after the cake, telling her he'd let Matt know about the thing with Melanie.

Humiliation and then a sense of betrayal rushed through her. How dare he? "You did what? How could you do that, Nathan? If I'd wanted him to know I'd have told him myself."

"He needed to know, Tate. He loves you. He wants to protect you."

She narrowed her eyes. "I don't need anyone to protect me, Nathan. I can take care of myself." No one else ever had, she could count on herself, damn it. Melanie was a stupid bitch and Tate had handled her.

"You don't need it but you deserve it. I don't feel bad, honey, so spare me the look. It hasn't worked on me in ages."

"It worked on you Thursday, Nathan, when you were arguing with William."

He tried not to laugh but he couldn't help it. "Okay, okay, so it still works. Tate, I love you. You don't know how much. I'll never be able to put into words how much you mean to me, not in a million years. He wants to be part of your life, why hold him out?"

"What's going on?" Beth approached and Nathan sighed.

"Nothing." Tate waved it away. The last thing she wanted was to bring any drama to the Chases' grand living room.

"I told Matt about what happened with Melanie."

Tate gasped and then growled at him. He had the good sense to look worried.

"Well good. I don't know why Tate hadn't before now."

"I'm not having this discussion. This is *mine*. It happened to me. Not you, not Nathan, not Matt. You don't own it and it's mine to share or not. You don't get to make my choices for me. No one gets to make my decisions for me but me. You had no right, Nathan, and you've made me look like a pathetic fool." He took something and used it against her. Matt would feel sorry for her and there was nothing worse than having someone feel sorry for you. Especially when she'd handled it and quite well she thought. Those women didn't make her feel bad, she meant it when she said she was better than they were. She was.

"Tate, you know I'd never...that's not what it was. I wanted him to know, to see you, to understand what you face."

"Damn you, Nathan! I'm not some pathetic little fat chick who needs crumbs from the table of anyone. I trusted you. You've humiliated me and I don't know if I'll share with you so readily the next time."

Anger burning through her, she hardened herself against the way his face fell at her words. Instead, she spun and walked away, out into the hallway. And straight into Matt. Could the night get any worse?

"I hear you had quite the little run-in with Melanie earlier this week. You planning to tell me about it before the picnic day after tomorrow?"

"Don't start on me, Matt. It's nothing and it doesn't concern you." If he hadn't been so angry at her for not telling him about Melanie, he'd have been amused at the way her chin jutted out and her eyes narrowed at him.

He grabbed her hand and tugged her outside onto the front porch. Cassie and Shane sat snuggled on the glider swing on one side so he hustled her to the opposite end, pulling her into the large chaise with him.

"Tell me."

"Matt, I told you, it was nothing and I don't want to talk

117

about it."

"Well that's not an option. You can't not share with me. I care about what happens to you. When I track her down I'm giving her a piece of my mind."

She stood, moving away from him quickly. "You will do no such thing! It's handled. I handled it. I don't need anyone to fight my battles for me."

"You may not need it but I do. I need to help you, to be a part of your life." He stood and she backed up a step. He exhaled with frustration. "Don't do that. I hate when you do that."

"I need to go." She darted to the side, toward the steps to the front walk.

"Oh no you don't, Tate Murphy! You can't run from me every time I get close."

Out of the corner of his eye, Matt saw Cassie stand and Shane rose shortly after that. Tate saw it too. Shane's size worked against them both in that situation.

"You going to stop me?" Tate's voice trembled a moment but steadied.

By that point several others had come out and at seeing Tate backed up against the porch railing and Shane and Matt looming over her, Nathan shoved them both aside until he reached Tate, pulling her into his arms.

"Get her things," Nathan said calmly to Beth who turned and went to retrieve their stuff. "Come on, honey, let's get you home. Why don't you stay at my house tonight? I'll even let you make me waffles tomorrow morning."

Cassie's hand caught Matt's elbow and pulled him back. When he turned to her, she shook her head hard, pain clear on her face.

"What the blazes is going on? Matthew, what have you done?" Polly came out and Beth moved around her, their stuff in her arms.

Matt hated that Nathan kept his body between him and Tate as he drew her off the porch and down to the sidewalk.

"I wouldn't have hurt her. I never..." Matt's voice caught.

"Matt, there's something so broken inside me. I know you wouldn't have hurt me but look how I acted. I can't control it. Just please, can't you see how wrong we are?" Tate's voice was thick with tears.

He moved toward her but Nathan shook his head and Cassie's fingers dug into his arm.

"Why are you holding me back? I can't let her go like this." He looked to Cassie, begging her.

"Look at her, Matt. Leave it. Let her get herself together. Let them help her. You can't fix her just now." Cassie's voice was thick with emotion.

Shane put his arm around Cassie and his cheek against her hair.

Polly looked to him and down at Tate. "Honey, please don't go like this. This was all a silly misunderstanding. Matt wouldn't hurt anyone, least of all you. He loves you. Let us be your family too."

"I know he wouldn't hurt me!" Tate cried. "Can't you all see? I can't even have an argument without turning into some kind of freak. There's something so wrong with me. Just please, leave me alone." She paused, looking at Matt sadly. Matt felt a sob building in his gut. "Get away while you can." She turned and let Nathan guide her down the sidewalk and help her into the car.

"Tate, I love you. You're not broken, damn it. You're

beautiful and wonderful and I'll call you tomorrow," Matt called out.

Anne and Beth got in the car on either side of Tate, both putting their arms around her.

Matt saw her body shake, knowing she wept. He had to lean against the railing to keep his knees from buckling as the car pulled away.

"Why the hell didn't you tell me she was abused?" Cassie asked softly.

"I don't even know the whole story! Bits and pieces is all I've heard. The dad is a drunk, the mom ran off a lot. They were poor, neglected. I don't know the extent of the situation. I know she's got major issues around eating because of whatever the hell the dad said to her and she took the brunt of a lot of emotional crap because she's not really his." Matt shoved a hand through his hair and began to pace. "I shouldn't have let her go. We could have worked it out."

"Matt, she was on the verge of losing it. Her family will know what to do."

"You have to help her, Cassie. Will you help her?" Matt pulled her hands into his.

She nodded. Cassie had been physically and mentally abused for several years by her ex, a man who tried to kill her twice. In the wake of a devastated medical career and no longer able to perform the complicated surgery she used to excel at, she'd become a victim's advocate.

"I'll try, honey. You've got to try and rein in your frustration when she flinches from you. It's not about you. She already knows it's bad, she knows it has nothing to do with you or how she feels about you."

Polly kissed Cassie's cheek before hugging Matt's side. "We'll all help her. She's a good girl. A smart one."

120

"Melanie started all this and I'm going to have a word with her about that." Matt wanted to shake some sense into his ex. How could she have been so stupid? And how could he not have seen what a horrible person she was while they dated?

"Melanie?" Polly's voice held warning.

He told them all about what Nathan had said and Polly was fit to be tied. "You leave that girl to me, you hear? The last thing we need is for her to spread rumors that a Chase boy threatened her. She and I will have a talk. Boycott my daughter-in-law-to-be's shop? I think not. Not if she wants everyone to keep shopping at her father's florist."

Edward laughed, the tension easing on the porch.

જી

Matt was pulling on his shoes when his phone rang. He'd left multiple messages for Tate but she'd shied away from replying. He knew from Nathan that she was all right. Mortified by her reaction at his parents' house and trying to process everything.

He left her a voicemail telling her he'd be picking her up for the July Fourth picnic at two. He planned to hash things out with her for a few hours before they met their assorted family members at the park for food and fireworks later on.

Half expecting it to be her trying to dodge, he was surprised to see Shane's cell on the display screen.

"Hey there," he answered as he stood to grab his keys and head for the door.

"Matt, Tate's at the hospital."

Matt sat down again. "What? Oh my God! Shane, is she all right? What happened?"

"I don't know everything. It happened at her parents' trailer. She's got a head wound. I'm on my way to the hospital just now. She's unconscious. One of my deputies is asking questions at the scene. I thought you'd want to know."

"Yeah. Yeah. Thanks. I'll be there as fast as I can."

He ran out the door, calling Nathan and getting voicemail. Getting the same from every other one of her siblings he tried. He called his mother and she told him they'd meet him there.

He burst through the emergency room doors and the staff directed him upstairs. Rushing up the stairwell three steps at a time, he saw her family, Shane and Cassie there waiting.

"What happened? Is she conscious?"

"My father happened," Tim said, his voice tight and very controlled.

"Your father put her in the hospital?" A sense of cold, deadly calm slid through Matt then. He'd never been one for fighting, always a kind of laid back guy but at that moment he was sure he could have beaten the hell out of Bill Murphy.

"One of their neighbors heard an argument. Nothing new. He called Tate because it got pretty bad. My dad and mom were on the steps, screaming at each other. He kept threatening to kill her.

"Tate went because that's what Tate does. Tate fixes things. According to my mother, Tate arrived and tried to calm my dad down. Told him someone would call the cops if he didn't stop yelling. She went up the steps to the little landing where he was standing. He pushed at her, to get her away and she lost her footing and fell back. She hit her head on the concrete pad the trailer sits on."

Nathan put his arm around his older brother and took up the story. It occurred to Matt that this probably wasn't the first time something like this had to be related to someone else.

"Head wounds bleed a lot. My mom saw it and yelled at one of the neighbors to call the cops. My dad took off."

"We were already on the way." Shane put his hand on Matt's shoulder. "Thank God, one of the neighbors had already decided things were too far gone and called 911. An ambulance got there right as we did and brought her here. We've got a warrant out for her father."

"Can I see her? Is she going to be all right?" Helplessness clawed at Matt, thoughts of her alone and hurt in the hospital bed filled his brain.

"She's unconscious but they said her vitals were good. I've had a few concussions. She's in for a long night of being poked awake every hour but Tate is strong, she'll be all right. Physically." Cassie smiled at him, squeezing his shoulder.

Matt swallowed and nodded. If he fell back on his professional training as well as the support of his family and his love for her, he'd be a bigger help to her.

"Where's your mother?" Matt looked back at Tate's siblings.

Nathan's mouth flattened and he shook his head. "She's at home. Apparently she told the cops she doesn't remember much about what happened even though what she told Tim was pretty detailed. Said she had to get out of town. She's more worried that she might have to testify and it'll put a kink in her social calendar than about Tate."

"I've got to see her." Matt had to hold it together for Tate's sake.

"Go on in." Tim nodded. "She needs you."

&

"Little Venus? Hey, gorgeous, time to wake up."

Tate opened her eyes and found herself staring into the most beautiful eyes she'd ever seen. Matt. Then the light brought a sharp new blast of pain to her head and she winced.

"What happened?" she croaked.

"Your father," he ground out through clenched teeth. "He was drunk and arguing with your mother. Threatening to hurt her."

"Oh that's right. I went up the steps to try and calm him down. His face was so red, I thought he might have a stroke or something. He turned to me, screaming, his hands waving all around. He went to push me back and I lost my footing and slipped. Hit my head on something."

"Yeah, the damned concrete. He could have killed you."

"Is he all right?"

"You're worried about him?"

"He was so red. It's hot. He was drunk, really drunk. Is my mother all right?"

"She's fine." Tate may have had a head wound but she knew enough to understand his silence meant her mother hadn't bothered to show up. Tate wished it didn't hurt as bad as it did, still these years later.

Matt brushed fingers up her arm. "Your dad left the scene. There's a warrant. Don't you feel sorry for him. Damn it, Venus. My brother has blood all over his uniform pants from where he rushed to you when he got there. Why didn't you call me?"

"He saw it?" She was horrified that Matt had been exposed to this part of her life and now Shane had been too? Great.

The doctor came in and pushed him out of the way to shine a pen light into her eyes and check her other vitals. Matt stood to the side, not letting her out of his sight.

"You're all right. Concussion. I told you the last time to

watch yourself. Ms. Murphy, your father—"

"Yes, I know, Doctor." Tate cut him off before he could say anything else but she caught Matt scrubbing his hands over his face. *The last time* echoed in her ears and she knew he'd heard it too. Shame, sharp and acute roiled in her stomach and she had to fight back heaving her breakfast.

"Well, you're going to have a shiner where the railing of the steps connected with your face when you went down. We're going to keep you here overnight for observation, you know the drill. Your eye is fine and the bruising should go away in a week or so. Your ankle on the other hand is sprained. You twisted it when you went down. You really shouldn't wear such high heels, they're murder on you."

"I like 'em and they're definitely murder on me," Matt murmured and Tate snorted a laugh.

Before leaving, the doctor said a nurse would be in within the hour and to ring if she needed anything. She did indeed know the drill.

Once alone she turned to him. "Oh fuck! Your family picnic. Go on, now and get going. I'm fine. I'll doze and be woken up repeatedly and you can call me tomorrow when I get home."

He shook his head and kissed her temple. "Tate Murphy, you are the dumbest woman I know. I'm not going anywhere. What kind of man would I be if I went to eat fried chicken and watch fireworks when my girlfriend was in the hospital? Plus, there's plenty of fried chicken here. Your whole family and mine are all in the waiting room. I doubt they'd let us picnic in here but I promise once I make sure it's okay, we'll get you a plate and you and I can snuggle and have our July Fourth lunch right here."

She started to cry. What had she done to deserve this man?

He took the hand what wasn't hooked to an IV, alarmed. "Venus? Honey, what is it? Why are you crying? Are you in pain? Should I call the doctor?"

"They're all here and I'm your girlfriend?"

"That makes you cry?"

"It's a good kind of cry. Answer me."

"Woman, I told your blonde ass I loved you over a month ago. Of course you're my girlfriend. You think I'd let just any woman make me scratch biscuits and cherry pie with fresh whipped cream? And I hate to say this, Venus, but only a man who loves you would stick around after hearing you sing in the shower. You're my woman. My heart."

She nodded, wincing a bit at the pain but happy. So damned happy. "Good. Okay then. Matt? I love you too."

She did. She always had in some sense as a fantasy but the reality of Matt Chase was beyond anything she could have imagined. Sweeter than her visual donut. He was special and there for her when she needed it. She'd have to worry about whether he'd bolt when he heard the full truth later. For the moment though, she let herself love and be loved.

At her admission, relief washed over him and he wanted to kiss her. Hell, he wanted to whoop at the top of his lungs, chide her for not saying so sooner, scoop her up and protect her forever and fuck her ten ways til Sunday all at once.

Instead, he sighed with a grin. "'Bout time you said so. I was beginning to think you were just using me for the sex. And where else would your family be? They love you too. And mine. As a matter of fact, they're all worried sick. Let me step outside and tell everyone you're okay. Your brothers and sisters are going to want to see you too."

"Matt?"

"Hmm?"

"Thank you for knowing they need to see me. Thank you for being okay with that."

"Honey, family is everything. It's one of the things I love most about you."

He walked outside and leaned against the wall, relief that she'd finally allowed him to love her and herself to love him warring with the rage he felt for her father. Bill Murphy would never hurt Tate again. Not while Matt had breath to draw.

Everyone looked up expectantly when he entered the waiting room. Marc, Liv, Kyle and Maggie had arrived. "She's awake now. The doctor came in and checked her out. She's got a shiner, apparently she whacked the railing with her face on the way down. A sprained ankle, you know the heels she always wears." He laughed, emotion still tight in his chest. "They're going to keep her overnight."

Shane put his arm around Matt's shoulder.

Tim and Beth stood. "Can she see people?"

"Yeah, I know she wants to see you all. They said two at a time."

"We've done this before." Anne sighed. "You guys go first. Nathan and I'll go next. Then William can go in. Jacob and Jill should be here in an hour or so. Go on, I'll call them and check in. Mom too, I suppose," she said. Tim and Beth nodded before going down the hall toward Tate's room while Anne headed outside to use her cell phone.

"You okay, son?" Edward asked.

"Yes, sure. No, no I'm not. Damn it. She could've been really hurt."

"Well, it's happened. You knew you loved her, but now you really *see* the power of what it means to love someone. A powerful thing, love. The power of the connection you feel but also the power of the fear of losing it," his mother said as she patted his hand. "Bend on down here and give your old mom a kiss. I'm proud of you. You have excellent taste."

Matt smiled and bent to hug and kiss his mother. "She told me she loved me."

Nathan grinned. "About time. I'm glad. You're good for her, Matt. But, you know this isn't going to be easy."

"Hasn't been so far. But it's been fun when I'm not scared to death."

"I'd like to see her too," Cassie said quietly, telling him with her eyes that she'd try to help Tate through the trauma if she could.

"Thank you, Cassie." Matt breathed a sigh of relief.

"We all want to see her. We'll wait for her kin and then we'll go in and let that girl know we love her too." Polly squeezed Matt's hand.

"Fine, that'll be fine, Momma. I'm here for the night," Matt said, distracted.

"You sure about that? You won't get any rest with them waking her up hourly," Nathan said. "We'll all be here if you need to get home for work."

"You think I'd leave her alone here? After what happened to her today? If she'd only called me before she went over there." He sat down, head in his hands. "Why didn't she do that?"

"Because, she's been handling my dad—and worse for most of her life. She's ashamed," Tim said, after coming out of Tate's room to sit across from Matt.

"I'm going to go in now while Beth's still with her. Tell him. It's been a secret too damned long," Anne said softly. Nathan kissed her cheek as she passed him to go toward Tate's room.

"It's not her fault, why should she be ashamed?" Matt didn't like feeling helpless and he really didn't like it that she'd feel responsible for being hurt by someone else.

Tim started to speak but he seemed so angry he had to shake his head and point at Nathan.

"Look, you have no idea what it's like to live in a family like mine. Your parents are educated, you grew up with money and prestige. Yours is one of the premier families in this area. You were all loved and cherished.

"My family wasn't. My mother took off for weeks at a time, leaving us with my father. It's no secret that he's a drunk, a mean drunk. He didn't work much so Tim and Tate had to take care of the rest of us. You can look at Tate and see she's not his, he knows it too. She embodied my mother's infidelity, a slap in the face every time he saw her."

Beth and Anne came out and Nathan stopped the story. "I need to see her. I'll be back in a few minutes." William joined Nathan as they went to Tate.

Matt heaved a sigh and Polly dabbed her eyes.

Beth settled in next to Tim and Susan.

Tim took a swallow of his coffee and continued. "So I'm big. Big like he is and after a few memorable knock downs with my dad, he left me alone, physically anyway. But Tate is small. I had to work, to bring food in for the others. She stayed at home for the kids, to take care of them that way. So the only way she could keep safe was to fade, to stay unnoticed. Other than me, she had no one who could protect her. She had to keep her focus on the little ones, he wasn't above hurting them to hurt her.

"I've seen your house at Christmas, by the way. All lit up with sparkly lights, that big tree in your front window. My house, our trailer, wasn't on the Petal Christmas lights map.

You think Tate's reservations about your differences are silly, I know you do. And I know it's because you don't know any better. But at our trailer Christmases were hell. Any excuse to drink more was a disaster. We didn't have a big shiny tree with loads of presents. We had one tree and my mother set it on fire to get back at my dad for something.

"My senior year in high school I only went enough to get my diploma. By then I worked two jobs and Tate did housework on the side for different families around town to bring in the money. I moved out and we brought all the kids with us. Tate finished school the best she could but worked every spare moment. Then she graduated and Anne did it, Nathan after her." Tim's voice broke.

Anne took over the telling and Matt realized what a unit they all were, with Tate at the heart. "We tried but we'd have fallen apart if it weren't for Tate. She missed a lot of school, didn't go to dances, didn't date. She dumpster dived for clothes even though it got her teased. But let me tell you, none of us missed school. She wouldn't allow it. She worked nights for Doctor Allen in Riverton so we could have healthcare." Anne worried her lip with her teeth. "Tate isn't heavy because she eats for stress or whatever, she's always been curvy, and our father would use that like a bludgeon. The stuff he says to her, it's repugnant."

"This isn't her first concussion," Cassie broke in gently.

"No. I told you, she was, is, his favorite target. Most of his abuse was verbal and emotional along with neglect. But when he got really drunk and if she was around..." Anne paused, taking a breath. Her hands shook and Tim ran a hand up and down her arm. "He broke her arm when we were in elementary school. She's had two concussions. He knocked her into a door when she shielded Nathan, she was like fifteen maybe? And another time, right after we'd moved out. Technically, Tim and

130

Tate had no right to take us. She paid him to let her bring us with them. She doesn't know we know that, it would kill her with guilt if she knew. She was late with the payments and he beat her pretty bad."

Anne put her hand over her mouth, unable to finish. Nathan rejoined them with William at his side.

"That's shame, Matt. Living with secrets, living with people who'd shake you down for money, people who harm you because you're the face of their failures. So no, she didn't call you. We were raised to hide it. Tate has lived her life for all of us, even for my asshole of a father and my waste of a mother. It's not that she didn't trust you to protect her, it's that no one has ever protected her ever. She's only had herself."

"She never said. I've asked her about it but she wouldn't talk about it. I knew it had to be sort of bad, but why didn't she tell me?"

"Jesus man, have you not heard a thing we told you? She's *ashamed* of it! She's afraid you'll judge her, the way people have judged us all our whole lives. Deal with it. How does one tell someone they've been abused anyway? Is it appropriate between courses at dinner? After a picnic? How should she have told you and how would you have reacted? She's afraid of letting anyone in, because people hurt her or they ignore it when she's hurting." Nathan shook his head sadly.

"Good Lord," Polly whispered, holding Edward's hand.

"If you're going to leave her over this, please do us, do her a favor and wait until after she's recovered and home," Beth said.

"You think I'd walk away from her because of this? God, what kind of man do you think I am? I love her. I wasn't making that up. She's...in the months we've been together, she's become so much to me. I would never hurt her, especially not over something that wasn't her fault."

"We'll be her shiny Christmas mornings," Polly said quietly. "We've got room around our tree for fourteen more."

Matt kissed his mother, fighting back tears. "Thanks, Momma. Why don't you and Daddy go to see her while I get myself together."

His parents nodded and headed down the hall. Matt stood and faced her siblings. "Thank you for trusting me to tell me this and for helping me to understand her better."

"We trusted you with the story because you seem worthy of her. Please let us be right." Anne stood and hugged him.

"I love Tate with all that I am."

His siblings and their wives surrounded him, hugging him.

Shane looked into his face. "You gonna be all right? We've got your back."

"Yeah, but thanks. Thanks to all of you."

"It's gonna be hard to make charges stick if the mother won't *remember* anything. If he says it was an accident they may not go forward. It's not my choice, I want you to know I'll do all I can, but you should be ready for that eventuality."

Matt sighed, swallowing hard. "We'll handle it if it comes along. Maybe the mother will do the right thing."

Shane's face told Matt just how dubious he was at that idea.

Matt's head spun. He didn't quite know how to process all he'd heard. He felt a deep, murderous rage toward Tate's father and bottomless tenderness toward his own woman. He knew he couldn't show her any pity or she'd be hurt. Knew she didn't want it, just his love and respect.

Tate looked up to see Cassie Chase come in. Deep, bone-deep exhaustion settled into her. She wanted to be that cultured, that beautiful and graceful, and that wasn't going to ever be. She'd never be tall and beautiful like Cassie.

"Hi, Tate, how are you feeling?" Cassie sat in the chair next to the bed and kicked off her shoes.

"Been better." She smiled weakly.

"Yeah, worse too, haven't you?"

Tate stilled as Cassie looked at her through alarmingly perceptive eyes. "I don't know what you mean."

"Yes you do. Takes one to know one, Tate. I've been there in a hospital bed after a man gave me a concussion. More than once as a matter of fact. I know the bitterness of shame in my gut, too. I know what it is to hide it and think people will judge. Do you know my story?"

Tate shook her head. "I know someone tried to hurt you a few years ago."

"My ex-husband. Tried to kill me actually. For the second time." Cassie told her the story of her years of abuse and of how her ex skipped out on his sentencing and then came to Petal to try and finish the job he nearly succeeded in before.

Cassie held up her right hand, the middle finger was bent at an odd angle. "This is what he did with the hammer. I'll never be a surgeon again. Funny how life works. Still, it drove me here to Petal, which brought Shane into my life and I realized what happened to me wasn't my fault. Wasn't my shame to bear and it's not yours either, Tate."

"I can't...how did you know?"

"I saw how you reacted after dinner the other night. I saw myself in your eyes. Heard more from your family just now."

Tate felt the heat of her blush, replaced by the familiar coldness of the shame. "They told you? All of you? They told you all of it?"

Cassie reached out and took Tate's hand. "I'm sure there's more. Years of shame. They told us enough that I know you were abused and still are. Enough that I know what an amazingly strong woman you are for stepping in with your younger siblings. You have a family with them. Your father tried to destroy it but you didn't let him. You win, Tate. That's what he hates so much. He can't break you."

Tears rolled down Tate's face. The wall of shame, the barriers that'd kept it all back were gone and it rushed out in wave after wave of emotion. Cassie got in the bed next to Tate, putting her arms around her.

"You win, Tate Murphy. Don't you see? You're worthy of all the people who love you. And let me tell you, your brothers and sisters love and respect you so much it made me proud to know you. And Matt, he loves you, Tate. It's not charity. It's not pity. He loves *you*. All of you, flaws and alcoholic father, neglectful mother, everything. Let it go and stop letting him get to you."

"That's so easy to say," Tate sobbed as Cassie continued to hold her. Wanting with all she was for it to be true.

"It is. Now. It wasn't just a few years ago when it was me in your place. I was a successful vascular surgeon, Tate! I had a good family who loved me, privilege, all the advantages in life and I ended up with a man who raped me and tried to kill me. I didn't deserve love. I didn't deserve a man like Shane. I didn't want a bossy, pushy control-freak cop who barely fits through doorways without having to turn to the side."

Tate couldn't help but laugh.

"I know. He's huge. Heh, yeah, that way too. But I digress. Listen, you, Polly is on the case so just give in. The woman will stop at nothing, you do know that? Matt loves you, you love him. He wants you and she'll stop at nothing until she helps him get you. And since you want him too, why fight it? Stop

Making Chase

letting your father control you. Stop going over there. If neighbors call, call the damned police. I promise you your father won't be shoving Shane around. You are not responsible for your mother and the life she's created for herself. You are not responsible for your father's pain that you're not his. It is not his right to harm you. Stop letting him control you. It's the only way you're going to heal and be free of it. And your siblings will follow your lead. They look to you for guidance."

"I have to eat with them at least once a year. For Jacob and Jill's loan stuff."

"Fuck that. Come on, Tate. Look, there are six of you and all the Chases too, we can come up with alternatives. It's one year. Don't let him control you this way. Let the people who love you help."

Could she believe it? Grasp the hope that she could have a normal relationship with Matt?

Matt tapped on the door, poking his head in. Seeing the state Tate was in, he rushed to her bedside, alarmed.

"Honey? Cassie, what did you do?"

"She just helped me. It's okay. Really."

"You're feeling better?"

"No. I have a horrible crying headache to go along with the concussion headache. My messed up childhood has been exposed to my boyfriend and his family without my permission and I've had a very emotional discussion with someone who knows where I've been. But I only have up to go, there's no more down at this point."

Cassie got up, hugging Tate carefully. "Please, give me a call or stop in at the bookstore if you want to talk. I'm trained as a victim's advocate but more than that, I'm your friend. I like you, Tate. You have excellent taste in shoes, I'm not sure if I told you that before or not."

135

Tate smiled. "Thanks. For everything."

"That's what friends, and family, are for." Cassie kissed Matt's cheek and headed for the door as Jacob and Jill burst in.

"Easy!" Matt grabbed Jacob before he jostled Tate.

Jacob winced. "Sorry. You okay? Tateness, I told you to stop going over there. Let the cops sort them out." Jacob kissed her forehead gently and Jill moved around to the other side, taking Tate's hand.

"If you just let them kill each other, we'd all be better off anyway," Jill mumbled.

Tate sighed. "Don't. Don't let them make you bitter. You're better than that. Now what on earth are you doing here? Jill, I know you had plans today with that new guy you're seeing."

"Shut up! My God, Tate, he could have killed you. You think making out and watching fireworks is more important to me than you are?" Jill looked offended but Tate saw the tremble in her bottom lip and knew she was about to lose it.

"I do think it's more important, Jill. Yes, I do. Damn it, they've disrupted our lives enough. I don't want him to do it anymore. Now get your butts back to Atlanta. Make out, watch fireworks. Use a condom!"

"I don't need a condom to kiss for cripes' sake! I've only known him a few weeks, he's not getting any just yet."

"Enough information, thank you very much. Tate, you're out of your mind if you think Jill and I are leaving before you get home from the hospital." Jacob crossed his arms over his chest and glared.

The nurse came in and frowned. "Too many guests. She needs to rest and you all need to let her."

"I'm staying." Matt stayed at her side.

Tate looked up at him and wondered why his voice sounded

that way. Was he trying to be alone to dump her? That was probably it. Loving a woman with some family problems was one thing, now that he knew the whole story surely he'd see how impossible it was for them to be together.

"Go on, guys. I need to talk to Matt and then I need to nap. You have the key to my place. There are leftovers in my fridge and clean bedding in the guestroom."

Jill kissed her cheek. "We'll get it ready for you to come home to. I'll stop by the library to grab you some books."

Jacob followed, kissing the other cheek. "We'll be back tonight. Rest. Love you."

"Love you both too."

They left and Matt settled into the chair next to the bed. Reaching out, she touched the softness of his hair for a moment and he leaned into her hand.

"They told you about my father."

He nodded. "Yes. God, Tate I don't know what to say it's so awful. I'm just relieved you're all right."

A tear rolled down her cheek. "I'm sorry. I didn't know how to tell you, it was embarrassing. You...you don't have to stay here anymore. I understand."

His eyes widened and then narrowed. "Good God, Tate, what do you take me for? Have I given you any indication that I'm that shallow a man? I love you, damn it. Not your father. You. I want to be with you and continue to build something with you. If you weren't suffering from a head injury I'd be offended."

"Matt," she sighed, "I worry that you'll regret this."

He cocked his head. "Why would I regret loving you? You don't seem to understand and that's my fault I suppose. Tate, I'm old enough to know what I feel. Old enough to know this is very different than anything I've ever felt before. It's you. You and me and it's right. Surely you can feel it."

"We come from very different worlds."

"So you keep saying. And I keep saying—so? Seriously. Yes, you had a fucked up childhood. One I can't even begin to imagine. But that doesn't mean we don't have a future together. Sometimes I'm going to do something stupid and thoughtless because I don't know any better. I'm a guy, it's what we do. And sometimes you're going to react in ways I don't understand and it's going to piss me off or confuse me. We'll get through it."

Tate put her head against the pillow and closed her eyes. He was fooling himself to ignore the real fact of the situation. People in town were going to talk. They already were talking. He'd always been on the inside, how was he going to take it when he risked that to be with her? Still, she was too damned tired to deal with it right then. And she didn't want to.

"Rest now, Venus. I'll be right here. If you wake up and I'm gone, I've just nipped out to get something to drink or to make a call to fill in your family or mine."

He kissed her forehead gently and she let herself fall into sleep.

∾

By the time they were ready to release her the next morning, his normally good-natured Tate was a very grumpy woman. He didn't blame her, they'd woken her up every hour on the hour and she looked dead tired.

He'd slept in her room all night, which meant he woke up every hour on the hour as well. And every three hours a new one of her siblings showed up and stayed in the room with them.

Shane had gone to Matt's apartment and packed him a bag, bringing it by the hospital. They'd found Tate's father and arrested him sometime overnight. Her mother had gone off to Dallas after trying to borrow some money from Tim, who'd refused.

Once the release papers had been signed, Matt and Tate got into a heated argument. He'd wanted to carry her to his truck and she'd looked at him like he'd lost his mind.

"I'll do the wheelchair thing like I'm supposed to but you're not carrying me." She slapped his hands away as he'd tried to pick her up.

"Why not? Tate, honey, let me help you."

"You're insane. You can push the wheelchair."

He growled at her and she raised a regal, white-blonde brow at him. Sighing, Nathan pushed his way into the discussion.

"As fascinating as it is to watch you two argue over stupid shit like this, let's motor. Matt, push the damned wheelchair, she doesn't want you to pick her up because she thinks she's too heavy. You, Tate, sit your ass down and shut up."

Tate did that cute little *hmpf*ing thing and Matt thought about arguing over how stupid it was that she thought he couldn't pick up a bitty scrap of a woman like her. He could carry two hundred pounds on his back up a ladder during a fire for God's sake, but she really was cute when she made that sound.

They got her settled in at her house. He tucked her into bed with some magazines while one of her sisters made tea. His mother had wanted to come over but already Tate's little house was bursting at the seams with Murphys so Polly agreed to bring over some food later that day.

Tate had fallen asleep by the time the tea had steeped so he left her to rest in the cool, darkened room and snuck quietly out to the living room where her family waited.

"Is she all right?" Beth asked, putting the tray with the tea on it down.

"She's asleep." Matt fell onto the couch.

"You need the sleep too. Do you need to go home? To work?" Tim asked from across the room.

"I'm good. I took the next three days off. I planned to stay here. Are you all okay with that?"

"More than okay with it. But one of us will stay here too." Anne drank some iced tea, rocking slowly. The house was shaded by several large willow and oak trees and the air conditioning kept it cool as well. Still, it was July in Petal and the heat rose from the pavement out front in dizzying waves.

"Mostly me, Anne and Nathan," Beth spoke up. "Jill and Jacob have summer classes so they need to go home and William and Tim have kids and wives."

"Hey, doesn't mean I won't do my duty here!" William grumbled. "She's mine too, damn it."

"William, we know that. She knows that. But you know how she is. She'd worry about Cindy being alone with the kids and you being here. She'd worry about you not being at work. She'll worry about Susan at the shop and Tim's business if he's not there. You can come by in the evenings. Back me up when I insist she take the rest of the week off."

"She can't mean to go back to work just yet anyway!" Matt looked at them all.

Tim snorted. "She'd have gone back today if we'd have let her. Tate views any kind of illness or injury as a weakness. She's the hardest worker I know. We'll have to wrestle her to keep her from going to the shop this week, crutches and all."

"She's going to do no such thing. She's got four stitches on the back of her head, she had a concussion, she doesn't need to cut hair just yet."

Beth waved it away. He recognized the gesture from Tate. "If you put it that way she'll go back just to spite you. Anne and I have worked the schedule out. We've got it covered until Monday. That gives us four days. Let us handle that part. Although I like that you put her first. I like that a lot."

Pride swelled through him that her family approved.

He excused himself, going into her room and closing the door. Quickly stripping to his boxers, he carefully slid into her bed, pressing himself against her before dropping into sleep.

Chapter Nine

Tate chafed at the way her sisters watched her so closely. Every five minutes someone shoved a glass of water or some fruit at her.

"I'm not made of glass!" she growled through clenched teeth but Anne clucked and continued to hold out the glass of iced tea.

"It's that mango green tea crap you like so much. Shut up and drink it or I'll tell Tim you're not taking care of yourself. You weren't even supposed to come back to work until Monday. We agreed to let you work today because you said you'd take it easy."

"Oh for heaven's sake!" She took it and sipped. "Thank you. Now go see to your client please, mine is coming in two minutes and I need to take a pit stop."

Tate hurried off but when she got back she recognized the lacquered blonde head sitting in her chair. Her eyes met Polly Chase's in the mirror and there was no escape.

"Hello, honey. How are you?" Polly turned to look at Tate better as she approached.

"I'm fine, Mrs. Chase. How are you?"

"Well, just worried sick about you. But your color is back. You do have such pretty skin. I always wished mine was that creamy smooth."

Tate looked at the woman perched in the chair. Polly Chase was a total stunner for her age. Even with a hairstyle that predated computers. She was tiny but all around tiny. Petite little hands and feet, always wore perfect clothes. Tailored suits, pretty dresses, spiky stilettos. Her makeup was always flawless and her eyes, big and green, reminded Tate of late spring grass, vibrant. Tate would have bet her entire year's salary that Polly Chase never envied anyone's skin, much less hers.

"Mrs. Chase, I'm beginning to see where Matthew gets his gift with stretching the truth."

Astonishment showed on Polly's face a moment and then she laughed, delighted. "I sure do like you, Tate Murphy. Now come on over here and do my hair and we'll talk about my son. And you'll call me Polly."

Anne met Tate's eyes as she passed and they both had to hold back a laugh. The woman was totally incorrigible.

Beth gave Polly a shampoo and brought her back to Tate's station. "I'm going to go ahead and pretend I don't know Anne normally does this so you can grill me on my intentions with your son. Would you like some tea?"

"Yes please. And I do so love it when people let me boss them around. Makes a small woman feel mighty, know what I mean? Of course you do, you've pretty much raised your brothers and sisters. I see the way they are with you. A gift, having people love you so much, being part of something that means everything."

Tate felt something click inside her at that moment. Polly Chase understood her better than anyone had, more than Matt, more than her own siblings. She met Polly's eyes in the mirror

143

briefly before beginning to towel and blow her hair dry. As she got the extensive backcombing and spraying process started, she had to wrestle back her emotions. Other than her siblings, when had an adult actually cared about her? Reached out the way Polly was doing? That broken little girl inside Tate's soul wanted to grab it, take the hand Polly held out because damn it, she needed it.

"It's all right, honey. What *are* your intentions with my Matthew then?" She knew. The amazing thing about Polly Chase was that she saw that little girl inside Tate and didn't run. She *wanted* to comfort her and know her.

Polly sat back and Tate began to talk about Matt.

As Tate worked on her hair, Polly absolutely fell in love with Tate Murphy. She loved all her daughters-in-law but none of them had ever really sat down and talked about her sons with her the way Tate did.

Tate loved Matt. Not his name, not his looks or his money, she loved his laugh, the way he pitched in when anyone needed anything, the way he took care of her after the hospital. So many people looked at Matt and saw a pretty boy who had it easy, they didn't see the rest of him, the compassion and love, the way he threw himself into everything he truly cared about. Tate saw that and Tate loved him for it. And Polly loved Tate for it.

The girl was fragile in many ways but she'd always be a good partner to her son. Polly would never tell anyone, but she'd always worried about Matt the most. He seemed so carefree and easygoing but he wandered around looking for something to challenge him. Women were easy, too easy. Which is why he never kept one very long. She'd had hopes for Liv, thought Matt was a damned fool for letting that one go at the time but now she knew Liv was for Marc. But Matt had started drifting again after Liv. He needed something to work for.

He did have it easy in other ways too. He'd been tested at school early on and scored off the charts, got that from his daddy. He'd never gotten less than an A in a class all the way through school, scored outrageously high on his SATs and then rejected college. Broke Edward's heart that none of his boys wanted to go into the law.

But underneath it all, Matt wanted to make his own way. When he'd started the fire academy, Polly had known it was the right choice. Yes, he'd been at the top of his class but he'd had to work for it. And when he was out on the job, he worked, he had to focus and give it his all and that made it perfect for him.

He'd been fulfilled by his career and it made her and Edward proud to see Matt come into himself as a man through his job. But still, no challenges in his personal life.

Until Tate.

Polly watched Tate as she worked on her hair and laughed, talking about Matt. Who'd have thought it would be this girl who stole her son's heart? Matt had squired some of the most stunning women in the area around. None of them had been right for him and Tate was beautiful in a different way but it wasn't apparent at first glance.

"So, tell me, has Melanie been keeping up with her nasty little campaign?"

"Blunt. What if I said I didn't want to talk about it?"

Polly thought about it for long moments. "Well, surely it's your business and all. But you should know right up front that no one messes with me and mine. Certainly no twitterpated piece of fluff like Melanie. And make no mistake, Tate, you're one of mine. All your brothers and sisters and their children are too. I don't take kindly to anyone threatening Matthew's

145

sweetie. And I really don't like her attitude about you and your background." She met Tate's eyes straight on in the mirror. "Because money doesn't give you class or pride and your address or your parents don't make you better than anyone else."

"That's not true, Polly. You and Edward made your sons better men."

Oh. That tore at Polly because the girl meant it and that was a shot straight to her heart. Reaching up, she took Tate's hand and squeezed it. "I do believe that's the best compliment I've ever received."

"Melanie hasn't been back but several cancellations called up and rescheduled. Thank you."

"Don't thank me. I don't like that sort of play on class differences. It puts my back up. I wasn't raised that way, my boys weren't, it offends me. Girls like Melanie after my boy offend me. You are coming to dinner tomorrow night, right?"

"No, Mrs....Polly, it's family dinner at my house this week. Last week at your house was pretty disastrous, I wasn't sure you'd want me back. I'm sorry. I didn't get a chance to apologize for making a scene."

Polly saw the girl go pink. "Tate, I understand there are reasons that made you react the way you did. Matt, like his brothers and his father, is a very protective man. He wanted to help you when he knew you'd been harmed. You know that I expect, as well as you know he wouldn't ever hurt you or try to control you. We all have buttons, honey. Yours got pushed. It makes you human. Why don't you all come to my house tomorrow? I'll put an extra leaf in the table and we'll eat in the formal dining room. We've got room for an extra dozen. Your brothers and sisters and those children are always welcome."

Beth strolled past and waved hello. "Afternoon, Mrs. Chase.

No offense or anything, but you're going to find it a hard proposition to talk a Murphy out of a dinner where Tate cooks. It's the highlight of the month, those Sunday dinners at her table."

"I'd heard you were a wonderful cook, Tate. Good enough to give me a run for my money even." She winked to let the girl know it didn't make her angry. "Tell you what, we can cook something together. How does that sound?"

Tate was quiet for a bit as she continued to do Polly's hair.

"Tate, honey, it's no secret my son loves you. He wants to be with you and eventually, our families will have to merge more. Why not start now? In fact, why don't we eat at your house this time, trade back and forth."

"Polly, my house bursts at the seams with fourteen as it is. But we can do something out back since the weather is so nice. It's a huge yard with lots of shade. Play equipment for the kids although Nicholas isn't quite big enough for most of it just yet. I don't want Liv to be outside in the heat, though, being as pregnant as she is."

The girl was really a miracle.

"Livvy loves the heat, unlike Cassie and Maggie." Polly chuckled. "But if we make it after seven when the sun is going down it'll be fine. I worry that you're taking on too much though so soon after the hospital. That's ten extra people."

Tate stepped back and looked at Polly's hair, making sure it was even. She patted it and handed Polly a mirror.

"You did a great job with that, honey." Polly spun the chair and checked out the back.

Tate wanted to offer her the chance to change it with a new look but women like Polly identified strongly with their hairdos and Tate didn't want to upset that applecart. Polly Chase had a strong enough sense of identity that she could ask for something new if she wanted it.

Tate was scared shitless over the idea of having ten Chases at her house. Her little house. But Polly was right, Tate and Matt had gotten a lot closer since she'd returned from the hospital earlier in the week. Things between them were serious and if she meant to go on with him, they would have to bring their families together. It didn't make sense to keep them all apart when both Matt and Tate were so close to their families.

"Well, if you'd like, you could come over early and help me cook." Another woman in her kitchen, an alpha woman like Polly would be a challenge but Matt was worth it. Family was worth it.

Polly grinned. "Why that'd be lovely! I'll come over at say, five? What are you planning to make? I'll bring over some of the ingredients. No, don't argue, you can do the same next week when you come to my house. Since you're such a fabulous cook we can share duties. If that's okay with you?"

Tate took a deep breath and let it out. "Sure." She told Polly her menu plans and the two of them worked out a grocery list and a schedule.

ઓ

Tate got out of her car and froze as she saw who stood on her porch, leaning indolently against the railing.

"What are you doing here?" She stood by the car, not wanting to get any closer to the man who'd landed her in the hospital just days before.

"I'm out on bail. Seems the prosecutor believes my story that it was an accident. Your mother had a convenient memory lapse as well. I thought I'd come here to mend some bridges."

Her father's smirk belied his words.

She leaned against the car, arms crossed over her chest. Nathan would be by in fifteen minutes but if she had to, she'd get in the car and drive away. She was done letting him hurt her.

"I'm not interested. Just go home. And don't call me to fix your problems with my mother anymore." Her voice shook a bit but it was a step.

"Well and see, here I was about to congratulate you for landing yourself a man at all, especially one with a wallet like Matt Chase." He took a step off her porch but she put a hand out.

"Stay back. Don't get any nearer."

He stopped and jerked his head to the side. "I didn't come here to touch you, *daughter*. I had no intention to have you fall down those steps. I don't care enough about you to harm you."

"Could have fooled me all those times you did harm me. Now what do you really want? We both know you're not here to mend anything."

"Money. You have it, I don't. Give me some."

A sick feeling twisted through her. "Ah yes, I should have known. I suppose a job is too much energy to give when you could drink all day instead? How about I pay for rehab? You know I will." She hated that she wanted to help him, he didn't deserve it but she couldn't make herself stop being concerned.

"I don't need a job now that my daughter has her own business and a rich boyfriend, now do I? The way I see it, Tate, is you landed him, God knows how looking the way you do. And I should benefit from that. I supported you and those other brats, I should be reimbursed for that."

Incredulousness rode her. "You did *what?* I'm not arguing

with you. Nor am I giving you a cent. I work for my money and I don't take anything from Matt. I don't need to. We both *work* for a living. You ought to try it."

The thin veneer slid off his face then and the man she'd feared settled into his features. Nausea threatened but she held back.

"Let's put it this way then, Tate, since you're being so ungrateful and all. I'm thinking I'd love to be part of your new life. Turn over a new leaf. I'd love to get to know your new family. Since I have so much time and all, I thought I'd come over more often. Maybe stop by the firehouse and visit with my daughter's new beau." He shrugged. "Or you can give me a few hundred bucks and I'll keep scarce."

She sighed. The Chases seemed okay with her past but that was when they didn't have to confront it face to face. How would it be if her father just showed up at Sunday dinner, drunk and belligerent? How would Matt feel then? And how would her brothers and sisters feel when they'd finally had a good life?

She'd gone to the ATM earlier to give Nathan cash and her grocery list. She dug into her purse and pulled out three hundred dollars cash and thrust it at him.

"Take it and don't come back."

He took his time, leisurely coming toward her and grabbing the money. Tucking it into his pocket, his smile made her sick. "Thank you, *daughter*. Now I'll be on my way, not to bother you again."

Nathan found her rocking in her chair, still sweating from throwing up. He knelt in front of her. "Honey, Tate? Are you all right? Do you need to go back to the doctor? Is it your head?"

She shook her head slowly, wanting so much to tell him what happened. He'd understand. He'd hug her and tell her it would all be okay. But after that experience with the whole Melanie thing, she knew he'd also want her to tell Matt. Or worse, tell Matt himself. He'd also tell her to stop giving their father money and she couldn't do that.

She finally had something real with Matt and no one was going to threaten it. She was the only one who stood between the ugliness of her father and the beauty of her family. She had to protect them as she always had and now that Matt was hers, she'd protect him too.

"It's the heat. I'm all right now. I made you a grocery list but I forgot to get cash."

He waved that away. "Not a big deal. You never let us pay for anything and I'm bored with sneaking money into your purse when you aren't looking." He cracked a smile and she snorted. They all did it. She just put the cash aside and used it on the kids or to make special treats for them.

They were safe from their father. She could handle him and keep him away from everyone. She'd done it most of her life and she'd keep doing it now.

"Let me give you a check." She moved to rise but he put a gentle hand on her shoulder to stay her.

"I mean it, Tate. No. You don't know how happy it makes me that you're letting me do your grocery shopping. So let me. It's some groceries. Considering how much I eat over here, it's a bargain for me. I'll be back in a bit. Matt should be here in a while right? You want me to stay until he gets here?"

She smiled, love flooding through her. "I'm fine. I managed without a keeper before Matt came along. I need to call William about the tables and extra chairs anyway. Bring back something you want me to make for dinner. You can stay can't you?"

He laughed, dropping a kiss on her cheek. "What a

question. I'd love to stay. I'll be back as soon as I can. I'll have my cell but I'm betting you'll have another Murphy or two over here before I get back anyway."

She wanted to tell him about their father but she couldn't explain how she knew.

When he left she called William and he promised to bring over a few extra banquet size tables and chairs early the next afternoon.

Making up her mind, she called the police station.

ℂ

"What do you mean they let him go?"

Matt heard Tate's voice rise and he hurried through her front door to see she was on the phone.

"Yes, yes, well isn't that nice? Perhaps someone would have seen fit to call me, you know, the person who got a concussion and spent the night in the hospital? No! If someone had called me would I be calling now? Oh fuck me! Listen here, bub, do you think I give a rat's ass if someone in some other place should have called me? I didn't get called."

Matt exhaled sharply. They let her father out of jail? He pulled his cell out of his pocket and dialed Shane.

"Yes, I know, she's yelling at one of my deputies right now. I'm sorry, Matt, it's up to the prosecutor's office to call the victim and we didn't know she hadn't been informed," Shane answered before Matt even said a word.

"They let him go?"

Tate turned and saw him there on the phone, he stepped to her, kissed her briefly and they both went back to their calls.

"The prosecutor isn't going to prosecute. He said it was an accident and Tate wasn't that eager to testify. Matt, the mother is backing up his story."

Matt's stomach dropped as he looked up at Tate who was apparently hearing the same thing. She mumbled her thanks and hung up the phone.

"Shit. I have to go." Matt wanted to make it all right for her, damn it.

"I'm sorry, Matt. I know where you are right now. Believe me. Come talk to me when you can, okay?"

Matt agreed and flipped the phone shut.

"They let my father go. They're not even going to prosecute him." Tate's voice as she spoke to him trembled slightly.

He embraced her gently, stroking his hands up and down her arms. "I know, I was just talking to Shane. I'm sorry, Venus."

"My mother is backing him up. And it was an accident. I don't think he deliberately tried to hurt me. He was gesturing all around. I yelled at that deputy. I need to apologize. It wasn't his fault."

A bubble of hysterical laughter hit Matt and he let it go. Only Tate would be concerned about that right now when the man who'd hurt her was out free.

She called and apologized to the deputy as Matt got them both some tea. He didn't like how pale she looked. Nathan came in with groceries some minutes later and Beth followed soon after.

Tate perked up as she started to make a chicken salad for dinner. She didn't even rely on the crutches much by that point as she hobbled around her kitchen. It seemed to him that merely taking care of other people made her feel better.

As they ate, she told him about the combined Chase-Murphy dinner the following night and he grinned. His mother never ceased to amaze him. Then again, neither did Tate. Twenty people was a big chore for a woman who'd just been in the hospital, but if his mother agreed to it, he knew she'd make sure Tate didn't overdo it.

After dinner, Beth and Matt did dishes while Nathan took out the trash and Tate folded laundry. He realized how normal it felt, being there with her in her little house. How quickly they'd moved to this level surprised him but he wasn't scared.

"You don't need to stay over, Nathan. I'll be here and I have tomorrow off so I'll help in the morning to make sure she doesn't overdo it." Matt looked around the corner where Beth helped Tate put clothes away before telling Nathan about their father and mother.

Nathan slammed a fist down onto the arm of the couch and Tate came rushing out. "Nathan?"

"I'm sorry, honey. Matt just told me about Mom and Dad."

So much for talking quietly and in private.

Beth's eyes widened as she demanded an explanation and she began to pace when they gave it to her. "She's out of her damned mind. Well, that's it. Tate, no more. Don't you dare go over there again. She's made her bed and so has he. You can't fix them and it's just going to hurt you. We don't need them anymore. We'll figure out what to do with Jill and Jacob. It's just one more year."

"Amen. Now, Tate needs rest. We'll see you both tomorrow afternoon." Matt ushered them both out and came back to find Tate pouring herself a drink.

"You want one?"

"You sure you do?"

She turned and sipped the amber liquid. "I'm not him. Yes, I grew up with a man who used alcohol as an excuse to be a monster." She shrugged. "I don't. It's not an excuse but it's not evil either. It's just a substance."

Drawing her close he pressed his lips to the top of her head and breathed her in. "You're a very wise woman, you know that don't you?"

"Fuck me, Matt. Put your hands all over me. Make me come."

He stilled, wondering if he'd heard her correctly or if she was using an exclamation. He took her glass and placed it on the counter. A look into her eyes told him it was the former. "I'm going to lock up. I'll meet you in your bedroom in three minutes. Be naked."

Hurriedly, he checked the doors and windows and moved toward her room.

He halted in the doorway and watched her move. Graceful and feminine, she was so beautiful. She turned and locked eyes with him as she reached up to let her hair fall like a pale spill of moonlight around her shoulders.

Moving to her, he undid the straps of her dress and let it fall to pool at her feet. Her bra followed and she stepped out of her panties. He loved that she'd lost her shyness around him with regard to her body. He was glad she'd accepted how damned sexy she was to him.

"Take your shirt off. I want to see you, Matt."

He heard the urgency in her voice and it disturbed him. He traced her jawline with his thumb and she bit the fleshy pad when he moved over her lips.

"Are you all right, Venus?"

"I *need* you, Matt. Please."

His clothes were off in record time before he backed her to the bed and she fell back to the mattress, looking up at him, eyes shining with raw need, with something else he couldn't quite define. So he did all he knew how to do, ease that need, meet it with the same desire he felt for her.

Sometimes you needed to make love and sometimes you needed to be fucked. Tate needed the latter, needed every muscle in her body to know she belonged to Matt Chase.

She loved him so much it scared the hell out of her but she couldn't not love him. That he loved her too continued to awe her but she was done questioning it. She wanted to be with him forever and if he wanted that too, who was she to argue?

At that moment though, she needed him to want her. Needed his desire, his lust and attention.

Reaching out, she fumbled through the box in the nightstand and grabbed a condom. "On you. Now."

He grabbed it, ripping it open with his teeth and rolling it on in record time. When his fingers brushed over her pussy and found her wet and ready, a strangled moan broke from him.

"God, so damned hot and wet. You're so ready for me."

She reached down and guided the head of his cock to her gate and rolled her hips.

"Impatient," he chuckled.

"Yes! Where have you been the last ten minutes? Fuck me, buster!"

His only answer was a long thrust into her body that made her gasp his name as he filled her.

His eyes bored into hers, seeing so deeply that she wanted to weep with it and run away at the same time. It meant something to be known, to be loved despite what she came from, because of who she was. Emotion, deep and overwhelming, swallowed her, bringing tears to her eyes as she let her love for him flow from her, through her.

"Venus? Honey, am I hurting you?" He stilled and she wrapped her thighs around his waist and squeezed, pulling him closer to her.

"No. No, it's fine. They're good tears. I'm sorry." She laughed because he was so good, so fine and she was so damned lucky to be loved by him.

Leaning down, he kissed the tears from her cheeks. "I love you, Tate. I don't know what I'd have done if something happened to you. Seeing you in that hospital bed nearly tore me in half. You're so strong but damn, you're a tiny thing. Fragile."

"I love you too, Matt. And I'm fine. Fine here with you."

She squeezed her inner muscles around him and winked, breaking the tension.

His lips skimmed down her neck as he whispered endearments to her. His body slowly entered and retreated. Not fucking anymore, he made love to her with exquisite detail, kissing her, caressing her, telling her he loved her.

There was nothing but the two of them and that was all right. Better than all right, it was perfect and Tate couldn't remember another moment that was ever so perfect.

ॐ

Matt hauled tables and chairs along with Tate's brothers and his own as they set up in Tate's backyard. He loved her house and the giant yard out back.

Tate's nephew and nieces played on the playset, yelling and laughing in the early July evening and he realized just how happy he was. Satisfied. Fulfilled.

In the kitchen overlooking the yard, the women who meant the world to him laughed and prepared a meal while the men chased children and set up the tables. What an idyllic moment.

Edward stopped next to him, putting an arm around his shoulders. "You're good with this girl, Matthew. I like what she's done for you. I like this place. I like seeing our kin mix with hers. This is right."

Matt's heart swelled with pride at his father's compliments. "I was just thinking that. I love Tate. I think I started falling for her with the first bite of her cookies. But I hate that her father is out and I hate that threat."

Shane approached. "I'm sorry about that, Matt. I truly am. It wasn't up to me. If it had been, the bastard would still be in jail. I'm doubly sorry she didn't find out about it before he got out. I chewed the prosecutor's office a new one over that."

Tate had come out into the yard and lit citronella candles all around and plugged in the colored lights she'd strung through the big trees in the back near where they'd lined up the tables. The children laughed and she did too. She was damned good with kids and she'd be a wonderful mother. He froze a moment and then eased. She would be. And he'd be a good father too. He wanted to be with Tate every day for the rest of his life.

"Just hit you, didn't it? Saw her with your babies on her hip."

Matt looked at his father and laughed. "You're pretty scary sometimes, Daddy."

Edward shrugged. "I have to be. Your momma keeps me on my toes."

The women began to flow from the house with heaping platters of food, piling them from end to end across the three long tables they'd set up. Matt loved the way they all sounded, soft and light. He heard Tate's scratchy low voice and her laugh as it married with the sound of his mother and Tate's sisters. The thought that someone had just put her in the hospital less than a week before made him clench his jaw.

She was so damned precious to him. How could he protect her from her father at all times?

"It's hard. Getting past all the hurt she's been caused." Shane looked at Matt for long moments before his eyes moved to Cassie. Matt had watched as Shane learned more and more of Cassie's past, watched as his brother suffered over the pain the woman he loved had endured. And Matt had watched as Shane grew and matured into a man he admired deeply.

"But you will. And you'll need to let her let you in. Don't try to manage her, Matt. Be there for her but don't push."

"Yeah, 'cause you're such an unassuming, sensitive guy. What if she needs Matt to help her through things?" Kyle asked as he joined them.

"She's thirty-one years old. She runs a successful business. She and her siblings have supported each other through school. You saw how she dealt with this whole thing, how her family rallied around her. How she bounced back. She's not a mess. I'm just saying. I've been there."

Nicholas toddled over to Tate and she picked him up, kissing both cheeks and putting her own against the top of his head as she swayed side to side. When she opened her eyes, she looked around and saw Matt and her smile was for him.

"Thank you, Shane. Daddy and Kyle, you too. If you'll excuse me, my woman looks like she's going to leave me for another man if I don't get over there."

Tate held Nicholas against her as he played with her hair. Maggie laughed and said something to her right but all Tate was focused on was Matt. She smiled as he approached.

"Hey, you trying to steal my woman?" Matt asked Nicholas who just laughed and burrowed tighter against her.

"Mommy's getting jealous, Nicholas. Won't you come and give me some love?" Maggie held her arms out and Nicholas jumped into them.

Matt didn't waste any time, he grabbed Tate and hugged her before laying a kiss on those lips of hers. "I'm starving."

She laughed. "Sit down. Everyone, come on and sit down, dinner is ready," she called out and the seats around the tables filled quickly and food began to move around in an orderly circuit.

Damn his woman could cook. Matt sat back some minutes later and rubbed his expanded belly. "Woman, you're the best thing that ever happened to me."

He found her tell-tale blush charming even through the onset of food coma.

"I heard that. Tate, I have to tell you, girl, you're an awfully fine cook. That's not a compliment I give often." Polly put her head on Edward's shoulder, leaning into him.

Matt and the other men cleaned up while the women sat outside and watched the children play.

He felt like they'd taken a huge step with that dinner, one toward unifying all the things in his life that he held most dear.

Chapter Ten

Tate watched as Polly tucked a wayward curl behind Beth's ear as they sat around the table at the Chases for Sunday dinner. The two women laughed together and while it gave her great joy that they'd all been pulled into the Chase family with such ease, it also made her ache just a bit.

Polly Chase had become something more than the slightly scary mother of her boyfriend. More than the town matriarch and a client. She called Tate to check in on her day, sent over recipes and asked for Tate's. She picked up scarves and little knick-knacks she told Tate reminded Polly of her. Polly knew her favorite flowers and what kind of tea she liked.

More than that, she extended that maternal care to all the Murphys great and small. Her nieces and nephew were totally at home in the Chase backyard.

It was a revelation to Tate, that mothers like Polly existed. At the same time, it made her resent that she never had that. It wasn't like Tate to wallow but sometimes, at night in a small corner of her heart, she allowed it just a tiny bit.

As Liv's due date approached, Tate and her sisters were invited to the shower. It wasn't so much that Tate disliked Liv, in fact, Tate had always appreciated Liv's humor when she came into the shop. But now that Tate was with Matt, it was a reminder that Liv was everything Tate wasn't. And she'd been

161

with Matt. Matt had seen them both naked and it made Tate cringe just thinking about it.

Being around Liv now made her distinctly uncomfortable. She didn't want to go to the shower but it was unavoidable. She was Matt's girlfriend and a pseudo member of the Chase family and it was expected. And more than that, she didn't want to hurt Liv's feelings.

So she let Beth drag her out shopping. They found the place Liv was registered at and picked her up a few things. Money had been tight, her father had come by the week before and demanded five hundred dollars. His price rose each damned time she saw him. Still she didn't want to skimp. Liv was important to Matt and so she was important to Tate too. Even if she hadn't liked Liv herself, Tate would have gone out of her way for her.

At least the shower was at Cassie and Shane's. Tate liked Cassie Chase a lot and had come to consider her a friend independent of her relationship with Matt. She loved the way Cassie handled her dominating, burly husband. She even liked Shane, despite the fact that his size took some getting used to. And Cassie understood her in a way most other people she wasn't related to couldn't.

They stumbled in, trying not to gawp like hillbillies at the beauty of the house as they put presents on a table with the others.

"Hi, Tate!" Maggie came over and gave her a hug. Cassie, carrying a tray of food, grinned in their direction and called a hello.

"Can we help?"

Polly chuckled as she click-clacked over and pulled Tate into a tight hug and smooched her cheeks. "Come on out onto the deck. Liv's got her feet up and a slice of cake and she's not moving. Everything's done already so just enjoy yourself."

Tate smiled at Liv, waving. As they came out onto the deck she saw it was more than just Chases, there were several women she didn't know and a few she only knew by sight from school and town.

She felt fifty pounds overweight, three income levels too low and distinctly unattractive as the women sized her up.

"Hey all, this is Matt's sweetie, Tate Murphy," Polly called out to the crowd. She introduced Tate's sisters and she heard a lot of names and would remember a tenth of them.

Liv smiled up at her. "Hiya, Tate. I'm glad you're here. Come sit over here and let's visit."

Damn. "Sure." Tate sat and Polly shoved a glass of something pink into her hand and toddled off chattering and towing Beth in her wake.

"Why don't you like me, Tate Murphy?" Liv pushed her sunglasses up and looked Tate over.

Tate, startled, blinked quickly. "I...I do like you."

"I think you're the best thing that's ever happened to Matt. You're smart, funny, pretty, you care about him and his family. You're too good to be true but you don't like me much and it drives me nuts because I want you to like me. Is it that Matt and I used to be involved?" Liv motioned to her stomach. "Because as you can see, that's totally over."

Tate snickered. "Honestly, Liv, I do like you."

"Then what is it? You seem to get along with Cassie. Maggie, well she's like a bumblebee in a jar, she takes getting used to but she's all right. Me? You sort of skirt around. Have I done or said something to hurt your feelings? I'm sorry, pregnancy is making me even more mouthy." Liv's grin told Tate she wasn't sorry at all but it only made her like Liv more.

Tate sighed and thought honesty deserved honesty. "Look, you're, well, jeez, look at you. Here you are, tall and gorgeous, you dress well, have a lovely house, your body, even when you're pregnant is way nicer than mine. I can't compete with that. It's not that I don't like you. I do like you, it's impossible not to, which is intimidating in and of itself. It's that I'm *not* you."

Liv was quiet a moment as she nodded. "Well, the thing is, Matt doesn't want me. He didn't want me when he had me. Tate, he wants you. You. Thank you for the compliments, really. But maybe you don't see yourself clearly."

"You know what I like about people? When they don't bullshit me. I'm not all low self-esteem girl, but I can look in a mirror okay? I'm good for what I am, but I'm not you. And I don't see any point in pretending anything else. I don't have the time to pretend anything else. So pretty is as pretty does, and being smart and funny and having a nice face—all those things are fine. I'm good with who I am, but damn it, every time I get near you that seems to fly away and I feel fat, short and totally out of my element."

Liv cocked her head. "Fair enough. Every time I see the way Matt looks at you—even though I adore Marc with every fiber of my being and I love him more than anything but this tadpole in my belly—part of me twists because he's never looked at anyone like that. And then I'm so totally happy because other than Marc, he's the male I'm closest to in the world and he's found *the one.* He's one of my best friends and I want you to be part of that too. He loves you, you're the center of his everything and since he's my friend and my brother-in-law and since I think you're pretty damned cool, I want us to be friends. Plus, damn it, I want you to like me as much as you like Cassie. I'm shallow that way."

Tate laughed. "A lot of things come to mind when I think of

164

you, shallow isn't one of them."

"Oh, tell me more!"

Tate relaxed, even as she continued to catch a blonde woman about their age staring at her throughout the party.

"Who is that?" Tate asked Liv after the presents had been opened. She could hear cars pulling up and knew the guys had arrived.

Liv looked up. "Ah. Yeah. That's Sal. Don't sweat it. I wouldn't even have invited her but she works for Marc, takes on some of his clients who need nutritional consulting."

"And she's looking at me that way because she used to play naked with Matt."

Liv burst out laughing and the blonde looked at them again. "You know that's something you'll have to deal with, right? The ex-girlfriends buzzing around? All of us do. Maggie still has to and she's been with Kyle for four years now and they have a kid."

Tate nodded. "I know. At first it really sucked, but now I'm just sort of used to it. He never flirts back. He may be friendly but he never looks at them like he looks at me. I figure if I got upset every time I ran across someone he'd had naughty playdates with I'd be permanently pissed off."

Liv snorted. "Very true. And that's a great attitude to have. Because, and I've seen this happen three, no, four times now, when a Chase falls, he falls. There's no in between. They like a woman or they love her. Once they love her, that's it. Matt straying is not something you'll ever have to fear."

Some moments later, Matt came out onto the deck and as Tate's gaze was drawn to him, she noticed the blonde across the deck stared at him too.

"Still, I'm gonna be honest with you, Tate, 'cause I like you and all. I'm gonna look at him. Because he's mighty fine to look at." Liv took a look at Matt and then winked at Tate.

"Remind me to tell you about visual donuts," Tate murmured as she looked her man over. He didn't notice the other woman at all. His gaze scanned the deck until he found her and he moved straight to her. The fear edged away a bit as his eyes held nothing else but her. He sat, giving her a kiss as he circled her shoulders with his arm.

"Hey there, Venus. Man, I needed that." Winking at her, he leaned around Tate to blow a kiss at Liv. "How you feeling, gorgeous?"

"About a thousand months pregnant. Swollen. Sweaty. But I've convinced your lovely girlfriend here to like me. I feel much better."

Matt flicked his worried gaze back to Tate, who'd come to realize Liv Chase just said whatever the hell came to her mind. What wasn't to like about that?

"I told her I already did like her but that it sucked that she was all gorgeous and stuff and I was like a little blonde dumpling and you'd seen us both naked."

Matt paused, trying to figure out what the heck he could say and both Tate and Liv laughed.

Matt cupped her chin and brushed his lips over hers softly. Just enough to make her nipples hard and her pussy sensitize and ready for him. "Tate, I love you. You're beautiful. Liv is my friend but you're my woman. Do you understand the difference?"

She nodded enthusiastically and he grinned.

"Hi, Matt! Fancy seeing you here." The other woman had made her way over and sat, no, bounced her way into a chair across from Matt, her knees touching his.

"Well, Liv's my sister-in-law so I don't think it's that unusual I'd be here. I just came to get cake and steal Tate away. Do you know Tate Murphy?" He moved back a bit so their legs no longer touched.

"Yes, she used to clean our house." The blonde's voice went flat, snotty. "I think she does a better job cutting hair, or I hope she does. I go to Atlanta to do mine."

Matt blinked several times and sick humiliation seeped through Tate, replaced quickly by rage. Who did this woman think she was? But before she could speak, Matt did.

"What is it with people? You owe Tate an apology. You've just been really rude and I don't like it. Tate doesn't deserve that sort of thing and frankly, I'd have thought it was beneath you."

"Don't you care about what people are saying, Matt? *She's* beneath you. Look at her. Have some self respect."

"Sometimes. And sometimes I'm on top. And you're not. That's what bugs you isn't it?" Tate kept her voice low so Sal had to lean in to hear it. The other woman sat back and gasped but Liv laughed before getting serious again.

"You need to shuffle your ass on out of here right now, Sal. This is my party and Tate is my friend. I won't have her insulted by the likes of you and if you make me get out of this chair I'm gonna be even more upset." Liv sat forward. Seeing that, Marc hurried over and Tate wanted to crawl away. Every damned time she was with them, something dramatic happened. She should have just kept her mouth shut.

"I'm just saying what everyone is thinking, Liv."

"Everyone? I'm not thinking that. Are you, Matt?" Liv asked him and he glared at Sal and shook his head.

"What about you?" Liv looked up into Marc's face before looking back to Sal. "Because see, you might need a dictionary so you can look up everyone to see what it means. *You* might be thinking that. Melanie might be thinking that, but I'm not and I'd wager most people don't, especially those of us who actually *know* Tate so *everyone* isn't thinking it, Sal."

"Hey, beautiful, what's going on?" Marc put a hand on Liv's shoulder, caressing it. "Everything all right?"

"Fine. God, it's fine." Tate stood. "Liv, thank you for inviting me. If you ever need a sitter and Polly will let the baby out of her hands for five minutes, give me a call." She bent and kissed Liv's cheek but Liv grabbed one arm and Matt the other and they both hauled her back to sitting.

"You're not going anywhere, Sal is. She's insulted a friend and she's leaving, now." Liv turned her gaze back to Sal but kept her hand on Tate's arm. Tate felt the warmth of friendship in the gesture and relaxed a little bit.

Marc looked to Sal and back to Liv a moment. "Okay, Sal, you've upset my wife and my brother's girlfriend. I'm going to ask you to go."

Sal hurried out, mumbling under her breath and within three minutes more, her sisters and Polly arrived and the story was told over and over until Tate stood and made the *cut* motion with her hands.

"Enough! If one more person asks me if I'm all right like I'm a hunchback who lives in a cave I'm gonna lose it. It's over. I want it to stay over. Please. Now I really do need to get home. Thank you, Liv. It was a lovely shower and I'm glad we were able to chat."

"I'll drive you home. We can talk." Matt moved to the door with her.

"No. I drove here with my sisters. I'll get them home. Visit with your family. I'll talk to you later."

Nothing made him angrier than when she tried to pull

herself away from him like that. As if he were associated with those stupid people, or like he believed it. Well, as he'd done every other time, he simply ignored her attempts as he pulled her to him.

"You go and take your sisters home. I'll see you at the house in an hour. I haven't eaten. Won't you take pity on me and feed me?"

He loved the way she got flustered when he didn't let her win her silly attempts to hold him away. And when she knew he'd be licking her from head to toe when he saw her next.

"Fine."

He laughed, kissing her quickly, and walked her and her sisters to the car, seeing them off.

When he'd come back inside Liv had moved to the couch, her feet in Marc's lap. Maggie looked pissed off and Cassie was in a heated discussion with Polly on the deck.

"What the hell happened here?" Matt sat down across from Liv and Marc.

"It was fine until Sal came over. I can't believe that. I feel so bad." Liv's color had returned to normal but Matt didn't want her getting upset again.

"It's not your fault, honey. Tate doesn't blame you, I know she doesn't. I just can't understand all this stuff. Just a few days ago, Ron Moore cornered me in the hardware store about it. Some bunch of bull about Tate's mom and how I should watch my pockets. I've known this guy since third grade! He's met Tate one time and when I asked him for specifics he said he'd *heard it around.* Apparently Melanie has been saying stuff all over town." Matt exhaled sharply. "I didn't mention it to Tate so I'd appreciate it if none of you did either. Now what's all this about Tate not liking you?"

Cassie and Polly came inside.

"Tate and I had a very long talk, cleared the air. I've been dying that she likes Cassie better than me."

Cassie laughed.

"I still think she does, *hmpf*. But she's been feeling insecure about any comparisons between us and I've been feeling a bit, oh I don't know jealous maybe? Not like that." She looked quickly at Marc who rolled his eyes, apparently unconcerned. "But you know, you look at her in a way you never looked at me or anyone. It's hard at first. But she and I got past it and were visiting and laughing but Sal kept on staring. Lots of people stared. They're curious, Matt. Most of it wasn't hostile. You came in right after she'd asked about Sal."

"And you told her?"

"Look, Matt, it's no damned secret you tasted the nectar of many a flower here in Petal and the tri-state area. Tate's not stupid. But she wasn't upset about it either. She didn't like the attention but she laughed about it and it wasn't her covering up for being uncomfortable. She and I talked about the big issue for all Chase wives."

"Ugh, the constant female attention," Maggie spoke from the chair near the doors.

"Yes. But she's okay. She gets that Matt isn't interested in any flower in the garden but her." Liv shook her head. "But the thing with Sal wasn't just about her jealousy that Matt had settled down with one woman. This whole *oh there's an outsider in town, quick hide the silver!* thing is just weird. I don't know exactly what to do about this. But I do know we have to make a stand."

"Yes, we do." Polly sat down. "Cassie and I have been talking and we thought it would be good to make Homecoming our big exclamation point about Tate being part of our family. That is if Liv hasn't gone into labor by then."

"You'll have to excuse me if I most fervently hope to have given birth by next Tuesday much less two weeks from now."

They all began to plan.

&

"I can't believe that bitch!" Anne exclaimed as they drove away. "Sal has some nerve."

"Every fucking time I'm with the Chases some kind of drama ensues. It's downright embarrassing. I hate it." The fuck habit was back.

"It's not your fault, Tate. Sal was way, way out of line." Beth turned to her. "Don't let it get to you. That's what she wants. That's what they want."

"I've been thinking on this a lot. Matt was the last single Chase brother, they all wanted him. But you landed him. They can't stand it. In truth, they'd find fault with anyone who snatched the last Chase standing," Anne mused. "So screw them all. They can suck it. Who cares about them, Tate? You're the important one. You're the one he loves. You're better than the Sals of the world."

"Every time I'm with him in larger social settings I feel totally out of my depth. Beautiful ex-girlfriends every three feet. All his friends don't trust me and they talk about stuff I don't know a damned thing about. I'm not one of them and they know it."

They pulled into Anne's driveway. "Tate, Matt loves you." She shrugged. "He wants to be with you. You love him. I've never seen you so happy. Who cares about them? His family adores you. We adore him. It's all good." She hugged her before getting out. "I'll see you later. Call me if you need me. Love you."

Beth scrambled into the front seat and gave her basically the same speech when they arrived at her apartment complex.

She loved her family and she loved Matt but she hated the anxiety and didn't know what to do about it.

Some half an hour later, Matt walked through her front door, looking very intent. Without taking his eyes from her, he threw the locks and pulled the cord to the front blinds, casting the room into pale light.

"Bend over the couch arm, Tate."

Frozen, she stood and looked at his face, his features sexy, aggressive. Shivers worked over her at his manner, far more dominant than his normal laid back sexual playfulness.

Eyes still locked on hers, he pulled his belt loose, unbuttoning and unzipping his jeans, freeing his cock. One of his eyebrows slowly rose. "Tate?"

Stifling a nervous giggle, she shrugged and walked around the edge of the couch, bending forward over the arm. She closed her eyes when she heard the condom wrapper and felt the cool air on her bare thighs as he drew her skirt up to her waist and her panties down. She stepped out of them and let him widen her stance.

His fingertips drew a path up her inner thighs, brushing through the folds of her pussy, finding her wet.

"Just what I thought. I've been so damned hard since I saw you sitting there in the sun on Shane's deck, your hair gleaming in the sunshine."

The head of his cock found her gate and nudged into her body slowly. He made love to her, his hands stroking over her back and thighs, his body pressing deep and withdrawing. Gently at first until the heat between them built and built to scorching and his speed increased along with the intensity of his thrusts.

One hand reached around and he found her clit, ready and slippery. She pushed herself back against his body, rolled her hips, wanting more and he gave it to her.

The fingers on her clit were slow, teasing and he brought her up, built her orgasm like a masterpiece and when it crashed around her, she had to yell into the couch cushion. The sensation was too much to bear, it drove her mindless, pleasure blind as the hand at her hip tightened and she felt the muscles in his abdomen grow taut and his cock harden impossibly.

"Matt, please. I need you to need me." She didn't know where the words came from but they came and brought a gasp from him followed very quickly by his orgasm.

Still breathing heavy, he kissed the back of her neck and withdrew, returning in moments, his pants still unzipped.

He looked pleasure wild, slightly feral and holy shit, he was hers.

Dazed, she managed to land herself on the couch and he sprawled alongside her, his head in her lap. Immediately, her fingers sought the softness of his hair as they enjoyed the silence for several minutes.

"What brought that on?"

He heard the amusement in her voice and was relieved he hadn't pushed too far.

Lazy, his eyes closed as he enjoyed the way she massaged his scalp, he smiled. "Dunno. I'd planned to waltz you into your bedroom and take you nice and slow but when I walked in the door and saw you, I had to have you right then."

"It was very inspired."

He laughed. "I'm glad you enjoyed it. I was concerned you'd be upset after the shower."

She sighed but didn't tighten up. "It's a cross I have to

bear, Matt. She's not the first, she won't be the last."

"To talk to you like that?" He sat up and faced her, his arm along the back of the couch resting on her shoulders.

"Yes. And I did clean her parents' house. I did a good job, even though my own house is messy, I work hard." Her chin jutted out and he kissed it.

"Who cares now? It's what? Fifteen years ago? Venus, some people live in the past. And I wish you'd tell me when people said things to you."

"Why, Matt? What could you possibly do except feel bad?"

"Why? So you're not alone in this. Do you think I like it that people treat you this way?"

"Do you think it makes a difference whether you like it or not?"

"Damn it, Tate. Why are you so hard sometimes?"

"Because people I don't even know stop me on the street to accuse me of trying to steal your money. Because your friend Ron cornered me at the public library to warn me that you'd see past a piece of ass soon enough so not to get comfortable with my newfound position."

Anger, hot and nearly unmanageable rose in him like bile. "He said what? Ron Moore said that to you?"

"Yes."

"Who else?"

"Doesn't matter. None of this matters. He'll only deny it."

"I don't give a fuck what he says. He's lucky if I don't knock him into next week for talking to you that way. Tate, I'm sorry this is so ridiculous. I'd say it doesn't matter but being treated that way does matter. What doesn't matter is anyone's opinion but yours, mine and our family's."

"I know."

He smiled. "You do?"

"Yes, I do. I know it's not easy, but I love you, Matt. I love being with you. If people don't like that, there's not much I can do about it but I'm not letting what we have go because people who don't know me don't like me."

"Yeah? Because Tate, let's move in together." He'd almost asked her to marry him but he knew it'd be too much for her right then. "I want to be with you every day. I want to wake up with you every morning."

"I don't want to leave this house. I love it here. And I'm not giving up Martini Friday with my sisters."

She was full of surprises, he'd thought they'd have to argue over moving in together. "Like I'm going to complain about a house full of tipsy, beautiful women. Although if we could plan it so you hung out at The Pumphouse first and invited Cassie, Liv and Maggie back here too, I'd like that a lot."

"I hate The Pumphouse you know. The last time you invited me everyone stared at me. Still, okay. For you. I suppose if we just came and sat with Liv, Cassie and Maggie, people will get used to it eventually." If Petal was meant to be the place they were to be together, she had to work harder to make it more of a positive place in her head. Let go of the past and build a future.

He kissed her. "Thank you. I love knowing you're there as I play pool. It's sort of sucked since we've been going out that you've been here when I was there. Speaking of that, I love it here too. Thing is, it's small for two people although my place is even smaller. But I have a suggestion. This is a huge lot. It wouldn't be hard to add on at all."

"I've been thinking about that for the last year or so. I'd be open to that."

"Who are you, ma'am, and where did you put my

175

girlfriend?" He leaned in to kiss her again and then once more, licking his lips afterward like she tasted good.

"I had this long talk with Liv and then with my sisters. I fucking hate how people react to this relationship and to me. But to give in and let them chase me off isn't who I am. I've been letting it get to me when there's nothing I can do to change it. All I can do is live for me. And for you. You say you want something with me. I want that too." She shrugged.

"Well to start, this dining room needs to be about three times the size it is now so we can have all the Murphys and Chases over no matter the weather. We need another two or three bedrooms and a den I think." He winked and they planned.

Chapter Eleven

Things began to settle in. That next week, Matt slowly moved his stuff into her house. She hadn't been too surprised to come home from work on Friday and see several sweaty Chase brothers with sledge hammers taking out a side wall to enlarge the kitchen. William and Tim were out there too.

"You aren't mad?" Matt asked as he came into the kitchen, freshly showered.

"We talked about this. You had someone come out here Tuesday to check the load bearing walls. You got the permits in next to no time, I'll have to thank Liv's connections with the mayor's office for that one I guess. You promised to do something and you're doing it. Far from making me mad, it makes me very happy. How long have you all been at it?"

"I got off at noon. Kyle had a half day and came with me. William showed up after he got off at two. Everyone else came as they got off work. We'll get a solid amount done tomorrow and Sunday too. But for now, it's time to play pool. Marc called to say Liv hasn't been feeling well. She'll probably have the baby any day now. Everyone has their phone on. But I'll stay away until ten since it's no boys allowed. In fact, we're all headed to Nathan's after pool."

She smiled. "Really? That's nice. I like to hear that you're all doing stuff together. And I know about Liv. I stopped by there on my lunch hour today to bring her a few things."

It was his turn to smile. "I like to hear that too. You're a good person, Tate Murphy. Oh and about next week."

She froze. *Homecoming.* A shudder of revulsion rode her spine. Tate dreaded it. Hated it with the heat of ten thousand totally clichéd suns. She'd been trying to talk her way out of going with the Chases for weeks but Matt would not let it go.

"So I ran into my momma earlier. She wants to know what we're bringing to the picnic next Sunday. And don't forget dinner at my parents' house after the game on Friday. I've already talked to Nathan and Anne, they're both coming and bringing dates."

She ground her teeth in frustration. The stress of this damned town event and her father's increased demands for money weighed on her more and more. He'd come back several times and each time he wanted more money. His behavior had deteriorated and he'd begun to threaten showing up at the kids' school in the afternoons, saying they should get to know their grandpa.

The thought of the way Tim and William would react to that little kernel kept her paying him. Her family was finally enjoying normalcy and she wanted it to stay that way. And once he found out Matt had moved in, it would get worse.

She'd had to juggle a few bills the week before to wait for payday, not easy when you own the darned business. But she had some money in savings if she needed it, which it looked like she did. And now the expansion of the house. It was a lot at once.

She knew it would get out of control. She knew that moment wasn't too far away and eventually she'd have to deal with it and tell someone. She couldn't afford to pay him forever.

But right then, she felt cornered by Matt's going around her to her siblings. "You did what? I told you I wasn't going to any of that fucking stuff. You know how I feel about Homecoming."

"Oh, *fucking* is it? What crawled up your craw?" He tried to tease his way into her arms but she slapped his hands away and took a step back. His grin slid off his face.

"What crawled up my craw? You went around me to Nathan and Anne to get them to go to this crap so I'd go too. That's what crawled up my craw. And it's crawled up your ass, not craw." She crossed her arms over her chest and glared at him.

"I did no such thing!"

She widened her eyes before narrowing them to angry slits. "Yes you did. I told you three weeks ago I wasn't going. And you acted like you didn't hear me. I told you two weeks ago, ten days ago, a week ago, three days ago, yesterday. And you thought, *oh, let's be sure Nathan and Anne are there so she can't say no.* Well I've got a news flash for you, tightass, I'm not going. You all have a good time."

"Why are you being like this? It's a damned picnic and a football game! My family loves to go, we do it every year without fail. You think you're too good for a football game?"

Hurt welled in her stomach. She put her shoes on and grabbed her purse. "If you think *I'm* the one who thinks she's too good for anything you don't know me at all. Go to your fucking snobby game and your fucking snobby picnic and while you're at it, try noticing for the first time in your shiny life just who *isn't* there. And you tell me it's *them* who feel too good."

She pulled at the door but he leaned against it, keeping it closed. "This is something you have to tell me, Tate. How can I understand if you don't tell me?"

"I have told you! I've told you six times I don't want to go. You don't listen. Now let me leave. I don't want to be here right now."

"Too bad because I want you here and I want us to work this through. This is our house now. Why don't you want to go?" He drew his knuckles down her cheek gently.

"Why do I have to give you an explanation to make it valid for you? Do I ask you for an explanation? When you say you don't want to do something do I make you? Do I demand you explain why? Do I disregard everything you say and try to manipulate you into it?"

He sighed. "No. You're right. I just want you to be with me. I won't go if you don't. It's a family thing, I want you at my side. You're part of that now. I want to show you off, I want to have you part of those memories. Please?"

His voice was so sad she knew she couldn't hold onto her anger any longer. Knew she didn't have it in her to refuse. She leaned her forehead on his chest. "All right. I'll bring baked beans and potato salad. I'm sure your mother is frying eighteen chickens and Maggie is making pies."

He tipped her chin up so he could see her face. "Your pies are better."

"I'm not usurping Maggie's spot. She's the one who makes pies and cakes and stuff and she's really good at it. Stop making trouble. You're very spoiled you know."

"I do. Thank you for agreeing to come. Will you make that pasta salad too? The kind with the feta cheese in it?" He fluttered his lashes and she sighed.

"Pushing your luck."

"I know. But I'll make it worth your while. We've got about twenty minutes until we have to go..."

She growled but allowed him to guide her back toward their bedroom.

ॐ

Hell had a name and it was the Homecoming game. Well, no probably the game was purgatory and the picnic would be hell. She could hardly wait to see.

"You look like you sucked on a lemon." Shane seated himself next to Tate and Cassie grinned around him, waving her hello.

"Do I? Because I was only thinking happy thoughts. Do you think I'll be able to fly?" Tate asked in a sing-song voice.

Cassie snickered and Shane allowed an upturn of one corner of his mouth.

Matt squeezed her against him. "You know how sexy I find it when you get all snarky, don't you?" he murmured into her ear and she laughed.

"It's hard to take a grown man who still wears his high school colors to a game seriously." She arched a brow at him and the green and white he wore.

Shane laughed aloud at that. He squeezed her from the other side, kissing the top of her head. "It's not that bad, darlin.'"

"*Hmpf.*"

But they'd surrounded her, blocking all routes of escape. Chases and Murphys all around her. Well, Tim and William had begged off, the traitors. They had wives and kids so they got to stay home. She'd get even for that. There were two drum sets with her niece and nephew's name on them for Christmas. She prayed Liv would hurry up and go into labor so they could leave.

It wasn't that she didn't like football. She did in fact. She enjoyed the game a lot. It was the atmosphere at the game she hated. Her kind had never been welcome at Homecoming events, that had been spelled out, bolded and underlined as she grew up.

She'd shielded the others the best she could, taking the brunt of the abuse but her memories of all the tears they'd shed over it still lay inside. Beth had told her it didn't matter now, that she'd made it all right and they'd be there for each other but judging by the hostile looks she was getting just then, it wasn't going to be an easy night.

"Walk with me to get some sodas and stuff?" Matt kissed her nose and winked.

Feeling claustrophobic and hemmed in by the wall of Shane Chase to her left, she agreed. He led her out and down the bleachers toward the concession stands.

Matt loved the way Tate looked that evening. Her hair hung loose, a wide, shiny red band holding it away from her face. Her sweater matched the band and the skirt was long and flowing, just to the ankles of the seriously sexy high-heeled boots she had on.

"Venus, have I told you how sexy you look tonight?" He stood behind her in the line, his arms wrapped around her shoulders, holding her to him.

"It never hurts to hear it again." She tipped her head back and looked up at him.

"Thank you for coming tonight. I know you're not thrilled about it."

"Yes well, I've thought of escaping but you've got my routes blocked. It's my only hope that Liv goes into labor tonight."

He laughed. "So charming. If I didn't know better I'd think you were avoiding my company."

"Order your stuff, goober." She indicated the window and he held her, one arm around her waist while he procured enough sugar, hot chocolate and food to keep the group happy.

They took the stuff back, arms full of food and passed it down the row before sitting down. Matt realized he needed to hit the men's room and excused himself. Kyle came along.

"Don't try and run for it, Venus," he called out, laughing as she gave him a subtle scratch to her nose with her middle finger.

Kyle laughed all the way to the head. "Your woman fits in just fine."

"She does and I think she's finally seeing that too."

"Matt!"

Matt turned to see Ron Moore approach with a few of their other friends. He narrowed his eyes and Kyle tensed too.

"Just the man I was looking for." Ron had the audacity to smile at him.

"Yeah? Why's that? So you could talk shit to me instead of harassing my barely five foot tall girlfriend in a public library like a pussy?"

"I see she ran right to you. I figured she would. Make herself look better. She's working you, Matt. What the hell is wrong with you?"

"Whoa!" Justin Fields, another friend stepped up and put a hand on Ron's shoulder. "Hey, what's wrong with *you*? What is Matt talking about?"

"This chick is working him for cash like a two dollar wh—"

That's all he got out of his mouth before Matt's fist landed square in his mouth.

Kyle waited until the punch landed before stepping in and pulling Matt back. "Okay, it's done. Let it go," he murmured in Matt's ear.

"Don't you ever, *ever* talk about Tate like that. You don't know what you're talking about. You've been my friend since third grade and you harass a woman you haven't bothered to get to know. Does it make you feel like a big man to terrorize women?" Matt stood over Ron as Justin helped him up.

"Tate's good people, Ron. What are you talking about? You're harassing her?" Justin turned to their friend.

"Melanie told me she was working you for money."

"Melanie is a jealous, bitter, angry psycho. I live with Tate, she won't let me pay half the mortgage. She's never asked me for money although she's made dinner for my entire family on dozens of occasions. She usually makes me go dutch on dates. Melanie has issues, Ron. She's taking them out on Tate."

"You don't know what she gets up to, Matt."

"Ron, you don't know her at all. What do you think she gets up to? She owns a small house, an old car and works sixty hours a week in her own business. When does she have time to work out of town businessmen for their wallets? Why don't you share with us just what you think Tate gets up to?"

"She's a gold digger. She's reeling you in for your money."

"You've said that and I've told you she hasn't asked for a cent in all the time we've been together."

"You're the fatted calf, which sort of makes sense since she's a cow. Shit!"

Matt hit him again.

"You said to tell you!" Ron yelled from the ground. Justin didn't bother trying to help him up and a crowd had gathered.

"I told you to explain your accusations, not insult my

woman."

"Holy fuck."

"Tate! Get back here," Shane ground out and Matt closed his eyes for a brief moment as he heard Tate approach.

"Just what the hell is going on here?" Tate demanded as she shoved her way into the group knotted around them. She looked at Matt and then Ron's face. "Did you hit this asshole?"

Matt couldn't help it, he started to laugh. "Why yes I did, Venus. Twice in fact."

She took his hand and kissed the knuckles. "He's not worth a hurt hand." Shaking her head she looked up at him. "What? Did you think I'd be mad because you punched him?"

Still laughing, he hugged her. "Of course not, Venus."

"Tate," Justin said, "I want you to know I don't think the same way Ron does. I think you're good people and I've never seen Matt so happy."

Matt lifted his chin at his friend in thanks.

"You've ended a friendship by believing someone who isn't trustworthy, Ron. If you so much as look in Tate's direction without an apology on your lips there's more where those two came from."

Shane finally pushed his way through the crowd. "What's going on here?"

People mumbled and began to wander off.

"Anyone see anything? Matt, you want to tell me why Ron is covered in dust and has a bloody nose?" Shane asked, stifling a smile.

"I think he fell," a passerby said.

"Yeah," someone else echoed.

"I fell." Ron brushed himself off. "Not a problem. Don't

come crying on my shoulder, Matt."

"I'd get a rabies shot if you're planning to hang out with Melanie much more." Tate turned her back on Ron and Matt kissed the top of her head.

Matt caught the speculative looks from other people as they walked back to their seats. Some curious, some approving and some angry. His glimpses into some of the ignorance Tate had to deal with were maddening.

Admittedly, it was a relief that he also saw friendly faces too. Friends who saw them and waved, people who were nice to Tate, genuinely accepting of her. He felt the steel of her spine relax a bit as they neared the row where their seats were.

The rest of the game passed relatively without incident but on the way to the parking lot, he noticed Tate protectively watch over her siblings and felt like a heel for manipulating her into coming. Fierce protectiveness burst through him as he watched her say good night to her brother and sisters. She was his and damn it, he'd make sure no one harmed her or made her feel wanting.

"I tried to hold her back but she caught sight of something going on and shoved past me. She's really fast, like one of those little dogs." Shane laughed as he kept his eye on Cassie and Maggie with Tate and her siblings. "I would have had to arrest you for assault you know, if Ron hadn't denied you hit him."

"Would have been worth it. Asshole. Called her a whore and a cow. He's lucky I only hit him twice."

"He said what? I'd have hit him too. Hell, I want to go find him and hit him right now. Why is everyone so hostile to her? She's so damned nice. Sweet even with that sharp sense of humor she's got. She goes to the damned old folks' home and cuts their hair for criminey's sake." Shane sighed.

"Some people get nervous and defensive when everything

they know gets threatened. It's easy not to think about class stuff when you come up where we do. Most of us, most of the people in this town don't care but there are people like Melanie who are only happy when they feel better than others. The stuff about her parents is a symptom. Essentially here's this outsider who came in and stole the last Chase brother. That's how they see it." Kyle joined them.

Matt shook his head. "It's like some stupid movie from the fifties or something. Honestly, it's totally unreal. She's been trying to tell me and I've been thinking she was oversensitive because of how she grew up." He paused. "She's trying to act like it didn't bother her but I know her. She's very sensitive, no matter how tough she tries to act."

"We'll make sure the picnic goes smoother. There's gonna be a lot of us. Put her near Momma. No one will mess with her then. Oh and Maggie too. We'll be on the outside. No one's gonna hurt her, Matt. We'll keep her safe. One thing we all need to keep doing is let this town and the people like Melanie know Tate is one of ours and we believe in her."

Matt didn't know what else to say. Family did what family needed to do. Still felt good though.

He caught up with Tate. "You still up to dinner at my parents' house?"

She sighed. "There's no choice. She's bound to have gotten at least five calls by now and she'll just hunt us down at home if we don't go over there and tell her the story firsthand. And speaking of hands, yours looks like hell. I want to clean it up better and I'm quite sure your mother has first aid supplies."

He grinned. "Come on then." He waved at everyone else. "See y'all in a few."

Polly met them at the front door, anxious. But instead of cooing over Matt's hand, she pulled Tate into a hug and it made her want to cry. She towed Tate down the hall and into Edward's study, closing the door behind her and leaving Matt in the foyer.

"Let it go now, honey. Give the tears up to me and be done with them," Polly crooned as she rubbed Tate's back.

As soon as Polly gave her permission, it was like her body just let it go and a sob so deep wrenched from her body that it buckled her knees. But Polly just went to her knees with her and continued to rock her and rub her back while she wept.

"It was wrong, Tate. What he said was wrong. What they've done to you is wrong. They're wrong. You're a good person. You love my son and he loves you. You're worthy of this wonderful gift you and Matt have. Don't you let them take the certainty of who you are from you. You're strong. You survived worse than those idiots in town who can't stand to see anyone else happy. You hear me? You give me those tears you've been holding back for so long and let them go. You're safe here."

So Tate let it go. Cried and cried and cried until there was nothing left and long minutes later, totally spent, she let Polly help her to the couch.

"I'm sorry. I didn't mean to fall apart like that. I don't even know where it all came from." She accepted a box of tissues and a glass of water from Polly who sat across from her and clucked. Her voice was rusty and every few seconds she hiccupped.

"It came from inside you. Where you've pent it up to be strong for everyone else. Tate, I know you, girl. You take everyone else's burdens for them. But you can only take on so much before it breaks your back. Sometimes you need to let it out. Tonight must have been very ugly."

"He called me a whore. A whore." Tate shook her head, still shocked. "I didn't hear it firsthand. That was the first time Matt punched him apparently. But I heard Matt telling Shane everything Ron said. Men. They must think we can't hear them at three feet away."

"They don't know we multi-task as well as we do." Polly nodded. "You're not a whore. He's wrong. You know that."

"I do. But it hurts anyway. He accused me of being a gold digger. Polly, I'd never use Matt for his money. Not ever. I've worked hard for everything I've achieved in my life. I love Matt, I'd never hurt him like that. Ever."

"I expect it does hurt, being misunderstood and misused. It's shocking to be faced with so much hatred. I know you love Matt. Matt knows you love Matt. Hell, honey anyone with eyes in their head can see you love my son. They are bad people. Wrong. The people in the world who count know the truth and that's all that matters. As for the rest of them? Don't let them see you hurt, Tate. They aren't worth it and you're better than they are. You hold your head up because you have every right to."

Tate nodded, blowing her nose.

"There's a bathroom right through there, sweetie. Wash your face and come out when you're ready. I expect Edward is holding Matthew back out there. Can I let him in? I know he wants to help."

Tate needed that, needed to see Matt, to be held by him. "Yes. Let me get cleaned up and I'll be out in a minute."

She went into the bathroom and looked at the ruin of her face. Her eyes were red and swollen as was her nose. Every last trace of eye makeup was gone or dripping down her cheeks. She looked like she had the starring role in a B-horror movie.

Still, after a few minutes of cold water compresses she began to look and feel better and she knew it was time to face the music.

The first gut wrenching sob broke Matt's heart. His father had simply put his arms around him and held him as they'd listened. Edward had urged him to let her cry it out, to let Polly mother her because she needed it desperately.

Matt wanted to rush in and take over, wanted Tate to open up to him that way but he understood Tate never would have let him bear the pain she held inside. Thank goodness his mother had been there and known just what Tate needed.

For long minutes she'd cried and cried and Matt had wanted to climb the walls. Her siblings arrived and they'd all stood in the hall and listened to her grief leave her body. Maggie held tight to Kyle, Shane to Cassie. The Murphys clutched each other and they'd all held vigil.

Twenty minutes later, his mother had come out and told them all very quietly that Tate needed a few minutes to clean up and to go on and get in the dining room. She sent Matt in to her, knowing they both needed it. Before he closed the door, Anne approached him quietly and said, "Melanie Deeds has a bill coming due." He couldn't have agreed more.

The door to the bathroom finally opened and her bottom lip trembled as she stepped into his embrace.

"Oh, Venus, I love you so much. I wish I could protect you from all this."

She didn't answer, instead just pushed herself closer to him.

After several minutes he kissed her gently. "You okay? Do you need more time or do you want to go and eat dinner?"

"I can't face anyone. You all must have heard."

"Heard what, Tate? Heard you being human? Heard you being mothered instead of doing all the mothering for a change?

We love you. I'm glad my mother could help and I'm sorry you had to see all that tonight. Come on, everyone is waiting and they want to love you. Let them comfort you for a change."

"They've all got enough to deal with."

"Tate, don't be selfish right now. They need to help. *I* need to know you'll lean on me from time to time. You take so much on, give us all the gift of being the strong ones every once in a while."

"You're going to make me cry again." The way she clutched his shirt made him want to keep her indoors and shield her forever.

"It's okay to cry you know. It's not a weakness."

She made her little *hmpf* sound and he knew then she was on her way back to being all right.

They walked out into the dining room and her siblings came to her, pulling her into an embrace. Matt put his arm around his mother and they watched until Liv burst in, pregnant and pissed as hell.

"Where is that Melanie and who's gonna hold my hair?"

Marc came in after her, grinning. "Liv's a little excitable after we got a call about what happened tonight. She wanted me to drive her around looking for Melanie but I talked her into coming here instead."

Cassie laughed and Maggie joined her as the three of them hugged each other and then Tate.

"If you'd just gone into labor early this afternoon none of this would have happened. Truly, Liv, I blame you." Tate blinked up at Liv, who laughed and hugged her again.

"I'm trying, sweet thang. Orgasms, spicy food, cod liver oil and this baby is blowing me off. Gets it from her father. Oops, did I say her?"

Marc burst out laughing as everyone excitedly discussed Liv's slip and the gender of the next grandchild.

Matt pushed Tate into a chair and made her a plate. "Eat it."

She shrugged, obeying him as she began to eat. Others noticed and began to fill plates and eat. His momma beamed at them all, doting over everyone, making Liv sit and get her feet up.

The dinner was a nice way to exorcise the demons of the evening. Being with family washed that all away.

ℒ

Back at home they'd just gotten out of Matt's truck when she saw her father lurking near the garage.

"I'll be in in a moment, I just need to get something from my car."

"I'll get it for you, Venus. What is it?"

"I need to be alone for a few minutes, okay? Please?"

"Honey…"

"I'll be fine. I just need to let this all go."

"You have three minutes and I'm coming back outside if you don't come in."

"I've lived here alone for the last several years. I can handle the driveway, thank you."

He smiled at her acerbic tone and headed inside.

She waited until he was gone before she charged over to the other side of the garage where her father stood.

"What? What are you doing here?"

"A fine way to greet your father." He stank of liquor and she fingered the pepper spray in her hand.

"Get the hell out of here. I have no money. I gave you all my cash. I told you, go away."

"Now that your boyfriend is living here, you should have more money coming in."

"I'm not letting him pay rent! What do you think I am? Her?"

"Don't you talk about your mother that way, girl," he slurred and moved forward but her anger over that evening spurred her on.

"Stop confusing her sins with mine. I have no more money to give you. If you push me too far and go through with your threats there'll be no more cash so shut up and go away until after payday."

She spun and stomped back into the house, triumph warring with fear.

She locked up and turned to see Matt leaning against the kitchen counter, looking at her speculatively.

"Who were you talking to?"

"Myself."

She bustled past him and took another look at his knuckles. "You really hit him hard. You're going to be sore tomorrow, it's bruising already."

"It was worth it. I don't scrap as much as I once did. When I was younger, my knuckles were nice and hard from duking it out with my brothers all the time. God, we used to be such a mess! Marc rarely got into the physical stuff but he used to work us all, set us up. He's a wily one."

Tate laughed. "Mindfucking. He and Liv really are perfect for each other. I used to think he was softer, more laid back but he's a lot more intense than he appears to be."

Matt nodded. "You're very observant. I don't think he understood that himself until he and Liv got together."

"Like you didn't realize how hard you worked until you got together with me? Or that you rode yourself too hard and thought you were shallow because a lot of things came easy?"

He started a moment and took a deep breath. She'd hit home with that one. *Good.* He needed some introspection too.

"Let's go to bed. Taking her hand, he drew her to their room and slowly undressed her before they settled into bed. She lay quietly, waiting as he stroked fingertips up and down her back while he thought about what she'd said.

"Most things have come easy for me. Do come easy I should say. Then I get bored and lose interest. I usually only stick with stuff that challenges me. Firefighting is one of them. It's a physical challenge every day and a mental one too. You have to be on your toes when you're at a fire or you'll get hurt. Hell, even if you're on your toes you can get hurt. But it's exhilarating, that work I have to put into it."

She stayed quiet as he processed. He liked that about her. She let him work through stuff without interrupting even though she had all that energy.

"And women? Well okay, that's been easy too. And so I suppose people have looked at me and thought I was a happy bachelor. I have been at times but really what I wanted was a woman who engaged me, challenged me, made me dig and work and be a better person and I never found that. Until that day I walked into the salon and you choked when you saw me."

He chuckled as he felt the heat of her blush against his skin. "I walked in there and there was this laughter. Feminine laughter, drew me right to you and your sisters. Pretty women, all of you. But I couldn't take my eyes from you. You were like this golden, shiny thing in the midst of my gray life. And you choked and got all embarrassed and then you teased me. When I teased you back you blushed. You are *real*, Tate.

"And I couldn't stop thinking about you and we started our lunches and I had to work to get to know you, to get past your defenses and every day I work because you make it worth my effort. Working to make a relationship is meaningful with the right person. It's not just something I do because I'm not quite bored enough to find something else. I wake up each day excited to work with you, looking forward to whatever new experiences we'll have, wondering what memories we'll create. I love you."

She snuggled close and kissed his chest. "I love you too. I was afraid at first. We're different. But you're everything a man should be and I'm so damned happy. You make me feel safe with you. That's not something I've felt a lot in my life. Excited, thrilled, desired, cherished, loved and safe."

He needed to hear that. It touched him deeply, soothed him. "You looked at me and saw past all the stuff most people see. That's...I don't even know if I have the words to express how much that means. I watched my brothers find the women of their hearts and I saw how that made them into better men, *whole* men but I didn't quite understand the process until it happened to me. You complete me because you love me. You *know* me, Tate. I'd do anything for you."

"Good, you can make me come."

He laughed, rolling her on top of him. "If people only knew the sex goddess who lurked behind those innocent-looking blue eyes of yours. Well, I'd have to beat them off with a stick."

"Mmm hmm. Put your money where your dick is then, bub."

And so he did.

℘

Tate was finally a part of something bigger than just her small universe with her siblings. When Liv went into labor some days after Homecoming and baby Lise came into the world, Tate was a part of it. Lise wasn't just the baby of someone she knew, Lise was a member of her extended family and she had to admit, seeing Matt hold the tiny baby made her heart sing.

Petal lost some of its unfriendly feel as Tate realized she had more there than she'd given credit for. She had friends other than her sisters for the first time. She had lunch with Maggie and Cassie, she visited at Liv's, checking in on her and the baby. She went on shopping excursions with Polly. The past was letting go or maybe, it was the other way around and Tate was letting go.

In any case, the only real dark spot was her father. His unrelenting presence in her life and the increasing weight of the secret she kept.

Halloween came and Matt began to suspect something was wrong. Tate was tightly strung, more than usual and she'd even let him pay for half the mortgage that month.

He'd confronted her about it but she denied there was a problem. She'd come home late a few times in the last few weeks, clearly upset and he had a feeling it had something to do with the things people had said around town.

It had died down a bit as they'd been seen more regularly and the Chases had so obviously taken Tate and her siblings into their family, making it clear they believed in her.

Fury rode him when he thought about her being talked to badly by people who didn't know what a remarkable person she was. If people couldn't look at Tate and see how much she cared about him, about her siblings, they didn't have eyes and they sure didn't if they couldn't see the way Matt looked at her right back.

They'd added on another bathroom adjoining the master bedroom, and another bedroom was being built to the other side of the kitchen. He found he loved coming home from work and making the place theirs. He also loved walking across the street from the station on the days he got off when she did, to come home with her.

Waking up with Tate nestled against him was the best feeling he'd ever had.

The weekend before Thanksgiving was the Harvest Dance at the Grange. A community fundraiser for the local food pantry and it happened to be one event Tate looked forward to.

Matt came home with a big white box and several smaller boxes, tossing them on the bed. "Just a little something, Venus."

She grinned. Still uncomfortable taking presents from him, it got a little easier each time and it made him happy to do for her and her happy because who didn't like presents?

He hopped on the bed and watched as she tore into the box and gasped, pulling out a beautiful deep blue dress.

"Matt, this is gorgeous."

"I thought it would look dead sexy on you. Will you wear it tonight? There are shoes and a purse in the other boxes. Anne helped me with them to be sure they matched and all."

"Yes. I was just trying to figure out what to wear and now I have the perfect thing."

How she loved watching him there, on the bed. On *their* bed, eyes lazily taking her in but she knew he paid attention to everything she did. It made her feel wildly sexy, the way he devoured her with his gaze.

They'd begun to make a life together in her little house. It was theirs now, getting bigger every day. The chaos of the constant construction was worth it to see the space grow into a home for them.

Having him there made her happier than she'd ever been, than she'd ever hoped to be. At first, she expected him to grow disillusioned or impatient with her family and other commitments but he didn't. He made room in his life for what was important to her and she found herself eager to do so for him.

Those times when they babysat for her nieces and nephew or Nicholas and baby Lise, she allowed herself to see their future as parents together. She wanted that with him very much.

Her father was a menace in her life, yes, but she'd do anything to protect this precious thing from his poison, from his evil, nasty darkness. She'd protect Matt because he meant everything to her and his family was too good to be sullied by the stain of her father. And she'd protect her own family too. At least he didn't physically scare her anymore although despite not wanting to care, she wished he'd get help. His drinking continued and in the periods right after her mother ran off again, he got worse. She wanted him to get better, wanted a chance to mend things but she knew it would never happen. So she held what was truly precious close and would protect it with her dying breath.

Matt watched her as she got ready. Hard didn't begin to

describe the state of his cock by the time she'd blotted her lips and turned.

"Man, you're the most beautiful thing I've ever seen," he murmured, putting his hands at her waist. So perfect. She was soft and sweet, curvy, feminine. Her breasts were showcased quite nicely at the neck of the dress and the skirt was full, coming to her knees. The shoes were sinfully high and whatever she'd done with her hair and makeup made her look glamorously pretty.

She blushed and he grinned. "Thank you. You do too. I love it when you dress up. I can't complain about you in jeans but in a suit? I'm not so sure I even want to leave just now."

"We could stay here. We could play senior prom. This could be the hotel room and we only have a few hours until you have to be home."

She burst out laughing and hugged him. "I love you."

"That means we have to go to the Grange doesn't it?" He pouted and she nodded.

"But only for a few hours. Lise is with Susan and William along with Nicholas. I'm absolutely sure Maggie and Liv won't want to stay too long. We'll make our exit when they do."

"Oh, good plan." He kissed her neck and twirled her. "Perfect. The dress is perfect for dancing."

"It's a swing dress, it's made for dancing. Good choice, Matt. Thank you for thinking of me."

Once at the Grange, they checked in at the table but quickly headed out to the dance floor. He loved dancing with her. She was so good at it, people often stopped to watch her. And with her heels she fit him nicely, soft against the hard wall of his chest. Perfect.

"Look at them. Goodness sakes, there's love for you." Polly

squeezed Edward's hand.

"She looks lovely tonight. In love too. I think moving in was a good choice. I know you want them married and having babies already but she's had a rough road to get to this point. She can see every day how much he loves her. How she fits into his life and his family. And people round town are starting to notice too."

"Mr. and Mrs. Chase, how are you tonight?" Melanie appeared at their table and Polly turned a narrow eyed gaze on her.

"Better once you move yourself away from my sight."

Edward smiled. "Now, lamb, I'm sure Miss Deeds here is only going to tell us she's been powerfully wrong about our Tate and how she's sorry she's been spreading such lies about her all over town."

"No, Mr. Chase, can't you see? She's a bad, bad person! She's had Matt move in to pay for her house. She's making it bigger on his dime. She's just using him. I loved him, I hate seeing you all taken in by her this way. She's a gold digger plain and simple."

Polly snorted and Maggie tossed a crouton at Melanie's head. "Hit the road, Melanie. You're an idiot plain and simple. Suck it up, Matt chose Tate. He broke up with you long before he found Tate. If you don't shut your mouth now, you're looking at a tableful of trouble. I promised to hold Liv's hair back when you got out of line again and she's still wild with pregnancy hormones."

Liv laughed and Marc patted her hand.

Cassie looked Melanie up and down. "What's your deal anyway? You're the nastiest piece of work I've seen in a long time. We don't like you. We think you're a hateful twit and Tate is one of ours. Matt didn't want you. There are other men in

Petal, not our men, they're all taken and we don't share. And we don't take kindly to our own being attacked by the likes of you."

"You girls scare me. I'm glad you're on my side." Shane winked at Cassie.

"Well, you've said what you needed to say and you're wrong of course. But you know that and that only makes you even more pathetic. As I told your mother last week. And as you've continued this nasty campaign against our Tate, it's been hard but I've had to shift my business to another florist cross town. Now, if you had any actual skills and say, a job or a business, I'd threaten that but you just live off your folks. Which sort of makes the whole idea that anyone *with* a job and a business the gold digger instead of you very ironic and ridiculous too. But I suspect you'd need a dictionary to know you were just insulted. So scamper along now before a drink gets spilled on you." Polly waved her away and Melanie stomped off with a wounded squeal.

The men at the table clapped and each woman gave a bow.

ဆ

"Matt, I think you should take the river road." Tate looked out the window at the clear night sky, the stars twinkling bright above them.

"Okay, anything for you, Venus."

She rustled around and held out her panties. "Good."

"Jeez, Tate, you're going to give me a heart attack!" He tried not to speed as he headed down the rural road that edged the river leading to the lake.

"Park, Matt. I can't wait much longer."

And she couldn't. Tate needed him desperately and she

wasn't quite sure why but he had to be inside her and as quickly as possible.

He pulled off, parking under an old willow tree and she turned, moving the dress out from beneath her as she crawled toward him.

Scooting toward her, he met her halfway and she hopped on his lap, grinding herself against him as he kissed her. His hand cupped the back of her head, holding her to him as he ate at her mouth, devouring her sighs and moans.

The other hand found its way under her dress and between her thighs. "Holy shit, you're scalding hot," he whispered into her mouth and she squirmed against his hand.

"Please, put your cock inside me. Please."

"You undo me when you need me so much."

She lifted up and yanked his pants open, freeing him. She slid the head of his cock through her wetness before guiding him to her gate and sinking down on him.

"What brought this on? Not that I'm complaining." He thrust up into her and she arched her back.

"I've needed you all day and we were rushed but dancing with you, your eyes on me all night, you're so fucking handsome and sexy. I just...yes oh like that...needed you so bad."

"Take your breasts out for me, Tate. Hold them so I can kiss and lick your pretty nipples."

She gasped softly and undid the side zipper enough to reach into the bodice and free her breasts.

Holding them out as he made love to her, his mouth torturing her nipples, cock deep inside her body, she felt like another person, a sexy person and she realized she was. He made her feel that way and she'd accepted it.

"Since your hands are busy, let me ease you some." Matt reached down and captured her clit between his fingers and squeezed gently over and over as she sped up on him.

"You're a sex goddess, Tate. So damned sexy I can barely hold on. I need to come so you have to too." He bit her nipple gently and then a bit harder and thrust deep, fingers still plumping her clit.

Tipping her head back, her back bowed as she came, the cab of the truck echoing with the sound of her voice and his whispered replies.

Chapter Twelve

Matt walked into a full house two days after Thanksgiving and caught part of a strained conversation between Tate and her baby sister, Jill. After they'd finished the renovation of the dining room, his parents had given them a nice, big table that filled the space.

Several Murphys and Cassie wandered around, gabbing and laughing. He loved that their house was a hub of activity. He caught sight of Liv sitting in the rocker in the living room, baby Lise a pink bundle against her chest, a shock of black hair peeking out from beneath a hat. She waved in his direction and he blew her a kiss and waved at Marc.

Tate stood in the kitchen, she hadn't noticed him just yet. Usually the moment he entered a room she alerted to his presence, their gazes meeting until they could make physical contact. He'd noticed her stress level had ramped up in the last two months but it didn't seem to have anything to do with their relationship. Still it made him nervous that something was clearly going on and she wouldn't share it.

Stress marked her face as she listened to her sister.

"They're books I need for this stupid final paper. I won't get the second part of my student loan money until January. I know five hundred dollars is a lot of money but I'll get it right back to you when I get the check."

"You'll have to give me a day or two. I don't have it right now. I have to move some money around."

Matt stilled. She hadn't said a damned thing to him about money trouble. They'd just paid off part of the renovation that they couldn't do themselves, several thousand dollars' worth. He'd wanted to pay it all himself but she wouldn't hear of it. So he'd told her it was much less than it truly was and taken on a far larger share without her knowing it. The last thing he wanted her to deal with was money trouble.

"Oh, I'm sorry. Tate, let me talk to Tim. I didn't know and I haven't even asked him yet. I just came to you and that's silly of me. You shouldn't be expected to do it all, all the time," Jill said.

And Matt agreed with that wholeheartedly although he'd never voice that to her. He knew what it meant to take care of family and so he never second-guessed how she dealt with hers.

"Can it not wait a day?" Tate sounded testy and it took him aback. She never spoke to her siblings like that unless they were fighting or nagging her about something.

"Sure. Tate, I'm sorry. I don't mean to make you upset." Jill wrung her hands and Tate saw it, pulling her sister into a hug.

"No, I'm the one who's sorry. I snapped at you and I've always told you and Jacob to come to me if you needed stuff for school. If you need it today, I'll give you my credit card number and you can charge the books that way. If it can wait until tomorrow, I'll get you cash."

Damn it. There was something wrong and she wasn't telling him. He turned before she saw him, catching Nathan's and Tim's eyes, motioning them outside.

"What's up?" Tim said as they walked out onto the front porch.

Matt told them what he'd heard.

Nathan ran a hand through his hair. "She takes on too much. I can swing the books no problem. I'll talk to Jill and Jacob, tell them to speak to Tim, me or William before going straight to Tate."

"It's more than that."

Both men looked to Tim.

"What do you mean?"

"Two weeks ago I saw her walking downtown, my father was headed in the opposite direction. Then I stopped in to get a haircut and I'd forgotten my lunch at home. Tate told me she'd loan me a ten to grab lunch but she had no cash in her purse. She got all weird about it. And with the first installment of the tuition this semester, she had to juggle for an extra few days. She wasn't late, but she's usually early and this time it was exactly on the day it was due."

"What the hell is happening and how is this connected to your...are you telling me he's working her for money?" Matt's anger simmered.

"It wouldn't be the first time. You know she paid him to let us take the kids when we first moved out. And over the years she's given him money. We all have I suppose but about five years ago he and I got into it and he won't come around anymore. He threatened Susan. Of course now apparently he's focused on Tate."

"And my guess is that Tate is taking this all and keeping it quiet to protect the rest of us." Nathan began to pace.

"I'll talk to Tate."

Nathan and Tim looked at him, pity in their faces.

"What?"

"Matt, you're hers now as much as we are. She'll protect you just like she's doing us. She's not going to tell you anything."

"I'm not playing this game." He leaned in and called to her. Surprised, she looked up and came toward him, the stress on her face smoothing as she got closer.

"Hi, whatcha all doing out here?" She joined them on the porch.

"Talking."

Her back straightened and one brow rose. "Want to enlighten me or is this a guessing game?"

"What's going on with your money situation, Tate?"

She took a step back and looked to her brothers who tried to keep stoic and tough but it didn't last long.

"My money situation? What do you mean exactly?"

"You know, I go out of my way to be honest with you, Tate. I know you're having money problems and so do Nathan and Tim. Tell us what's happening so we can help."

"Oh, you mean like how you told me Melanie came onto you at The Sands before the Grange dance when you were having lunch with Justin and some guys from work? Or about how you nearly got into a fight two weeks ago at the post office when you got lip from someone about me? Honest like that?"

Hell. How did she do that? Did Tim just chuckle? He glanced over and saw nothing but he suspected the line of Tim's lips might have curved up ever so slightly.

"That's different." He folded his arms over his chest.

"Is it now? How so?"

"Oh for fuck's sake! Knock it off. You're trying to muddy the waters, Tate. Give him a break. What is going on?" Nathan interrupted.

Damn, she had been. She was good, almost as good as Polly Chase. He'd let her push the argument away from the subject.

"Traitor. My money problems are no one's business. I just had a lot of stuff come down at once and I got a little overextended. It's not a big deal. In a few weeks everything will be fine."

"What's Dad's role in this?"

Matt had almost believed her story about a temporary problem until he saw her reaction. Her eyes darted away from Tim quickly and he saw her fists clench for a moment and then she smoothed them down the front of her pants.

"I don't know what you mean."

"Bullshit. Don't lie to me on this, Tate. He's working you for money, isn't he?" Nathan stood closer to her, grabbing her shoulders and Matt wanted to intercede but he saw it was necessary, saw Tate would protect them all unless she was made to reveal the whole story.

"It's none of your business!"

Her raised voice brought Anne out onto the porch and when she saw the scene she intervened. "Nate! Get your hands off her."

"Dad is working her for money. Has been for a while. Long enough that she's having trouble paying her bills on time." Nathan said it without taking his eyes from Tate's and Matt's simmering rage began to bubble.

Anne closed the door behind her and approached Tate, moving Nathan aside. "Honey, is that true?"

Tate's bottom lip trembled a bit but she didn't say anything.

"This is stupid." Matt grabbed her hand and spun her, putting her up on the porch rail so they'd be eye to eye. "You're going to share this with me, Tate Murphy because I love you and we cannot have this between us. That's what he wants. I won't let anyone hurt you, you have to know that."

"None of us is going to let you off this porch until you tell us what's going on," Anne added from behind them.

A tear broke lose from her eye and rolled down her cheek and he hated making her so upset. "It's nothing," she whispered.

"It's everything, Tate. Tell me. Share your burden with us. We love you."

She took a deep breath and told them. Told them everything from the first night until the last demand for payment of a thousand dollars.

"I couldn't have him harming you or the kids. Everyone was finally living normal, happy lives and I wasn't going to let him upset that. I'm not sorry!" Her chin jutted out and he shook his head, kissing it.

"You've had this weighing on you for five months now. Oh Venus, honey, no one should have to bear that alone. I've asked you if something was wrong and you told me no. Didn't you trust me?"

"It's not about that."

But in a way it was. She hadn't trusted him not to run off when faced with her father and that hurt.

He helped her down and kissed her. "I thought we'd worked through that. I thought you'd trust me to stand by you, to protect you."

"I do trust you, Matt. I just...the thought of him showing up at one of your mother's Sunday dinners, of what he is touching that just...I didn't want that to ruin what we have."

Her voice was quiet, but hurt that she didn't come to him still seeped into his gut. She'd been terrorized by this jerk and she hadn't thought enough of him to seek his help. Hadn't trusted their love and his commitment to her that he'd protect her.

"I have to go for a while. I'm hurt, Tate. I'm hurt you didn't trust me to stand by you."

"You're leaving?" Her voice sounded small.

"Not forever. I need to think. I'll be back." He went to his truck and as he pulled from the driveway he tried not to be affected by her face as she stood there, watching him drive away.

Matt sat at a table in The Pumphouse when Nathan stalked in. He picked up the beer and tossed it in Matt's face.

Shocked, Matt stood. "What the hell?"

"You asshole. You begged her to open up to you and when she did, you threw it in her face. You proved her right. You dumped my sister for sharing with you. Bravo. She's never, ever opened up that way to anyone before. I actually encouraged her to do it. I'm a fucking fool and you're an asshole. Your shit will be out on the street by nine tonight so don't bother my sister to come inside to get anything." Nathan spun to leave but Matt grabbed him.

"Wait! I didn't dump her. I just needed some time away from home. I'm not moving out!"

"Yes you are. Leave her alone, Matt. You blew it."

"That's my fucking house! You can't tell me what to do. Tate is my woman. I get that you're her brother and all but this isn't your business."

"It's my business when I have to listen to her cry. It's my business when she blames me for making her tell you something she didn't want to tell you to begin with because she wanted to protect you and the rest of us. You promised her you wouldn't let anyone hurt her and you did it yourself."

Matt reached out to grab his arm when Nate turned to leave again and Nathan shoved him back. "Don't touch me, asshole. I thought you'd be good for her. But you're just like the rest of them."

Shane came in and quickly moved to them. "What the hell is going on? Cassie called me and said Tate is holed up in her bedroom and her family is packing up your stuff. You broke up with her? Are you out of your mind?"

"Packing my stuff? I didn't break up with her! Why won't anyone believe me? Jesus! She holds on to this fucking horrible shit with her father for *five* months! She thinks I'd just walk away from her if her father showed up at my doorstep? How much trust does that show? Am I never allowed to feel anything? Only Tate gets to feel pain now? She didn't trust me to stand by her."

"No one ever has!" Nathan yelled it so loud and his words were so filled with emotion that everyone who hadn't already been watching the scene unfold stopped and turned.

"Yes, she should have told you. She should have told all of us but you can't know what it cost her to keep it to herself. Have you thought of that? How alone she must have felt as he terrorized her?"

Nathan took a step back and sneered at him. "Damn you, Matt Chase. This isn't about you, not in the way you think. I got more out of her, she's paid him seven thousand dollars. Why? Because she adores you. She loves you and she wanted to protect you and your family from the sickness we've had to endure our whole lives. From the *shame* of what we come from. Probably part of it was she was worried that when you were confronted with the reality of Bill Murphy you'd walk away. And until you've spent ten minutes with him, you can't possibly understand what a powerful motivator that is. He's..." Nathan shuddered in disgust, "...he's a horrible man. He's poisonous. She wanted to shield you from him. And not just you, he used everyone she wanted to protect, our nieces and nephew too because William and Tim are the ones other than her hurt the worst by my father. This isn't about her not trusting you, it's about her protecting you. That's what Tate does in case you hadn't bothered to notice."

Matt's head spun. He didn't know what to think. There was no question he loved Tate. He hadn't broken up with her, he just needed some damned time away to nurse some hurt feelings.

"She sold a bracelet I gave her two years ago to send Jill spending money. She dipped into savings to pay for the renovation but didn't want to take more because it's where she keeps the money for their tuition and any other emergencies. So feel your pain, Matt. You go ahead on. She told you she was broken at the very beginning and she is. But you're wrong to turn this and make it about you."

Nathan moved to leave but it was Shane who stopped him this time, looking back at Matt, who had to grab a chair as he took in the words.

"I'm not moving out. You can bet on that, Nathan. When I get back, Tate and I will work this out. This is not about you."

"Fuck you, Chase. For the better part of my life Tate took responsibility for me. Paid my father hush money so my siblings and I could live safely and be fed. That's why we're always at her house. She feeds us emotionally and physically. There's never a bare pantry at Tate's house, not in her heart or in her kitchen. This is about me because Tate is about me. Tate is more of a mother to me than the woman who gave me birth. I owe Tate everything I am and I won't stand by and let *anyone* hurt her. Not my father and certainly not you. Get out of my way Sheriff Chase unless you plan to arrest me."

Shane sighed and moved to the side. "Nathan, don't do this. Tate needs Matt, she loves him and he loves her. You know that. I know you're upset but you have to let them work things out."

Nathan said nothing more but left The Pumphouse.

"Whatcha gonna do?" Shane looked down at Matt.

"I'm going to go home and kick people out. Tate and I need to fix this without an audience."

"I'll go with you. I don't think it's going to be as easy as you think." Shane rode over with Matt.

"I just needed some damned time to nurse some hurt feelings. I didn't tell her I was breaking things off. I told her I'd be back," Matt explained to his brother after he'd told him about the payoffs.

"I understand why you'd be hurt, Matt. And I think Tate does too. But you're going to have trouble getting past her siblings who're all going to gang up to protect her from any perceived threat, you included. We'd do it in their place. I see their perspective very well. Cassie told me Tate walked past her and into her bedroom after you left, like there was nothing left to her."

"Damn it. Okay, okay. I shouldn't have left but..."

"But you felt like a failure for not protecting her. So you gathered up all your righteous indignation that she hadn't told you so you didn't have to feel like you'd failed the person who matters most."

Matt licked his lips as he turned down their street. "Yes. Shane, she's so small, she's mine to protect and cherish and I didn't. And she didn't trust me to."

"Do you really think that? Do you really think this was about her not trusting you to protect her? I'm not saying you don't have the right to be mad that she kept it to herself, I see why you are. But it's who she is. She's going to choose to take on burdens to protect people she loves. You knew that going in, Matt. If you can't handle that or this messed up family situation get out now. It's unfair to keep going with this relationship if something like this is enough to break you up.

"Worse things will happen. Loving someone means they can get to you in ways no one else can. There are going to be times you're so pissed off at her you want to rip your hair out, where you have to leave before you say something that'll hurt her. But you do leave, or you do take a deep breath and go get a soda because you'd rather hold back than harm her. That's what love is. And until I was with Cassie, no one meant that much to me other than my family."

"I don't want to leave her. I love her. I love being with her. I don't know what to think or feel or do. I've never felt so fucking scared in my life other than when I first got to the hospital in July when that bastard put her there. I wanted to be the one she turned to, the strong one. And when she did turn to me I ran. Fuck."

Shane snorted softly. "You'll both get over it. You'll work it out and the next fight y'all have you won't turn tail, although you'll make new mistakes because that's the way of it. It's not earth shattering. You had a fight. It happens. Now go in there and fix it because make up sex is the best."

Laughing, Matt pulled into the driveway and saw boxes of stuff stood on the porch and Tim sat out there with Beth.

"You need to grab your shit and go. We'll pay you back for the renovation when we can." Tim blocked the door.

"This is my house. I'm going in, Tim."

"No you're not. You've done enough damage." Beth shook her head at him.

"You're just making things worse. Come on, you know I love Tate. This is a huge overreaction."

"Overreaction? And you'd know this because you saw the damage you did first hand? Oh, no you couldn't have because you were off at your little bar drinking and looking at chicks." Beth's eyes narrowed.

"I wasn't looking at anyone. I'd never do that to Tate, and I'm not interested in looking at other women. Don't mistake me for your father either. I had *a* beer, most of it I didn't drink because Nathan tossed it in my face."

"You're right, the running off when things got hard thing is more like my mother. Hit the road." Matt hated it that Tim was so mad. He'd always considered Tim his greatest ally with Tate.

"Actually, this is his place of residence so he has a right to go inside, Tim." Shane, thank God Shane was there.

"I see, you're going to use the sheriff in your pocket to hurt my sister now?"

"Oh stuff it!" Cassie pushed her way past. "This has gone on long enough. Tate is worked into a frenzy in there and none of you are helping!"

"Of course you'd take his side."

"This isn't about sides! All of you get the hell out of here." Tate thundered out onto the porch, anger sparking in her eyes. She looked at her siblings and then Matt. "*All* of you. I want to be alone and I don't need or want anyone speaking for me, thinking for me or taking responsibility for me. How dare you all pack Matt's things and make that choice for him and for me."

Matt nodded. "They're just trying to help, Venus. They love

you."

"And you! You don't know a damned thing about it." She pushed Anne gently but firmly out and slammed the door, locking it. "None of you has the right!" she yelled from the other side of the closed door and turned out the porch light.

They all began to argue until Shane's cell phone rang. He answered, listened and started laughing as he snapped the phone shut.

"That was Tate Murphy, she's called the sheriff to file a noise complaint about a public nuisance in her front yard."

Matt scrubbed hands over his face. This had all spun out of control so fast. He didn't want to be arguing on her, *their* lawn, he wanted to be inside, holding his woman.

"Y'all go on home. I mean it. I'm going in there to work this out with Tate. If you love her like you say you do, you'll know she loves me and I love her too. We're gonna have arguments and she's going to be hurt and I'm going to be hurt. That's natural and normal and truly, no one deserves normal more than Tate. So go. Please. I'm sorry I've upset you all and we can all work this out later but Tate is in there alone right now." Matt sighed as he looked at the front of the house.

"Please," Cassie added. "Please guys. You know they're good for each other. I know you're hurting for her but you're the ones who started packing all this up. It wasn't her idea. She'd have done it herself if she'd wanted to. It's just a fight. God, if you all only knew how many fights Shane and I had our first year together. Okay," she grinned at Shane and he laughed, "still have. Tate is a strong woman and Matt's easygoing but they will have disagreements. If you gang up on him every time it happens, they'll never make anything work. Let them make up. If they don't, you know where Matt works. If you can get to him before Polly does, you can kick his ass."

Matt heaved a sigh of relief—ignoring the comment about his mother—his moving out hadn't been Tate's idea.

Her siblings moved and Matt nodded at them, reaching out and squeezing Cassie's hand when he passed. He unlocked the door and opened it slowly. When nothing took his head off, he went inside and found her scrubbing the tile in the bathroom.

"Hey, Venus. Whatcha doing?"

"Scrubbing the tile around the toilet."

He leaned around. "Tate, is that my toothbrush?"

"*Hmpf.*"

Ouch. "Oookay. Well, luckily there's a spare in the medicine cabinet then. Will you talk to me?"

"I already did."

"Tate, not that I don't like the view and all, your ass looks particularly lovely and I can see your breasts coming out the top of that shirt reflected in the shower door, but can we move this to the living room? Our bedroom? Someplace we can be face to face?"

"Matt, what are you doing here?" She turned and tossed the toothbrush, *yep his*, into the trash and took off the yellow rubber gloves, laying them under the sink.

"I live here. I told you I'd be back." He held a hand out to help her up but she ignored it and stood, brushing her hands off on the front of her pants and left the bathroom.

He followed her into the living room where she took the chair so he sat on the table, leaning in and taking her hands in his.

"I'm sorry you had to deal with this insanity with your father alone for all these months. I can't imagine how scared you must have been to keep it secret."

"Fine."

"*Fine?* That's it? Your fucking family moves my shit out onto the porch and you scrub the toilet with my toothbrush after you hide something important from me for *five* months and all you give me is an okay?"

"Who's got the fuck habit now, buster? Anyway, my family did that, I didn't. And what's more if you'd been here, they couldn't have done it now, could they? And don't you call them my *fucking* family, only I get to do that. I'm beginning to wish I'd fucking gotten in my car and headed to Atlanta for a few weeks like Liv did."

"And Marc went insane with worry!"

"Yes, because it's always about you people!"

"Back with that you people thing? Liv is from my side of town too!"

"Oh shut up! I mean you people with penises, not you rich people. God. Look, you *asked* me to tell you. I did. And then you ran off. You can't expect me to just be all, *hi honey, nice to see you, want a beer?* when you come back. You're the one who's always all, *I hate it when you try to run off* and then you did."

"You're right. I was hurt and I needed to be away from here for an hour or so. God knows why I imagined hell wouldn't break loose if I left."

"You left, Matt. When things got bad you left. I may have been wrong for not telling you, and I'm sorry I hurt you, I am. But I've been trying really hard to make a go of this. Even with all the insanity, even knowing you don't tell me everything to protect me, I stay and I try and today I trusted you enough to tell you and you threw it in my face and walked away."

"I felt like a failure out there on our porch this afternoon. You hid this from me when you should have been able to come to me and let me protect you. It shouldn't be the other way around."

Her anger softened and her eyes searched his face. "You're not a failure, Matt. My family is just too messed up. I'm messed up. You deserve more than that. Better."

"I want you to stop that talk right now. There's no breaking up here so quit it. I told you I'd be back. Okay, so I handled it wrong. I should have stayed and we could have talked it through without all the packing and yelling. But we're together, Tate. We'll work it out."

She listened to him and took a deep breath. The tentative smile fell away and her eyes narrowed. "Why do you stink of booze? It's hard to concentrate right now with you smelling like that. Bad memories I suppose but I'd really rather you not go out and tie one on when you're pissed. I don't mind drinking, I do mind coming back so bad off you smell like a brewery."

He laughed and then tried to get serious again. "Sorry." He put his hands up. "I'm not drunk. I had three sips of one pint of beer. Nathan threw the rest on me. Why don't I go shower and change and we can continue this?"

The corner of her mouth slid up a bit. "Nathan threw a beer on you?"

"Yeah. I thought he was going to pop me one and I'd have had to pop him back and you'd have been really mad at me for giving your baby brother a black eye. Luckily, Shane interceded so no blows were thrown."

"*Hmpf.* Go on."

He wanted to go to her and give her a kiss but his clothes stuck to him and now that she'd pointed out the smell it began to make him feel slightly nauseated.

"I'm saving the snuggles and sugar for after I'm cleaned up. But I've been running a tab."

When he finished showering he found she'd moved many of the boxes back into the house and was in their bedroom putting his clothes into drawers.

He approached her from behind wearing only a towel and put his arms around her.

"I could have done that." He kissed the top of her head.

"It gave me something to do. Anyway, my family made the problem, I'll undo it. They really didn't get most of your clothes. I was in here so they didn't touch what was in the closet and dresser. I think they took stuff out of the laundry. I'd done a load earlier today."

He turned her and his chest constricted a moment as he looked at her face, the features he loved so much. He could have lost her over something silly. That was untenable.

"First things first. Tate, we're going to fight sometimes you know. But unlike what Beth might think, I'm not your mother. I'm not going to abandon you. I shouldn't have left. I'm sorry. My feelings were hurt and I was upset with myself too, I needed a bit of space but I should have handled it differently."

He'd moved her back toward the bed and with a flex of his hips, bumped her onto the mattress.

"If I thought you were like my mother I'd have done more with your toothbrush than scrub the tile with it. I love you, Matt, but I'm not a doormat. Even if I gave in to my father, I'm not someone you can walk all over. I won't allow it." She put her fingers over his lips as he loomed over her. "But that's not what you did so calm down. I'm just saying that's not what you did and that's not who I am."

Frustrated at being unable to pull her T-shirt off, he grabbed hold of the neck and ripped it down the middle. "That's much better." He kissed the exposed mound of each breast and her skin broke into gooseflesh.

"I'm sorry I hurt you with this whole thing about my father. I would never want to make you feel like a failure. You're not.

You're my hero in so many ways. You do make me feel safe." Her voice shook and got breathy as he traced along the edge of her bra cup with his tongue.

He kissed her, nipping her bottom lip quickly. He sighed, rolling off her long enough to rid himself of the towel and start yanking on her jeans.

"Venus, I love you. We're together and we'll learn more about each other as we go. You *will* stop giving that bastard money, do you hear me? I *will* pay the next month's mortgage on this house. I've been here three months and you haven't let me pay my share. We'll work it out with your brothers and the school and with Shane to make sure the kids are safe."

"It's hard to concentrate when you're naked and ordering me around." She may have complained but she lifted her ass so he could pull her pants and panties off. She sat up, removed her bra and tossed the ripped T-shirt aside before pulling the blankets back.

"Tough. Now you're naked too."

"I noticed. Why are you over there?"

"I like looking at you laying there naked, your chest heaving because you want me so much even when your eyes are sparking at me because you're mad."

"You really should write all this stuff down. You could turn it into one of those books that teaches guys how to get a woman into bed. You'd make a million dollars. Oh and you're not paying my bills. That's not going to happen. Half the people in town already think I'm only with you for that. Although I question whether or not they've actually seen you because anyone with a brain knows I'm with you for the sex 'cause you look so good."

He laughed. His Tate was back. Their rhythm was back. Relief crashed through him as he knelt between her spread legs and skated his palms up her thighs.

"I'm paying *our* bills and I'm not arguing. I may be good in bed but I don't want to be a kept man." He winked at her.

"Well that's good since I've got three dollars to my name and you're worth way more than that."

He frowned. "Tell me you're going to let me pay next month's mortgage or there'll be no sex. I'll withhold it and everyone knows you're only with me for my cock."

"I don't want you to think I'm after you for money." She writhed beneath him though, grabbing the body part in question and squeezing lightly. He didn't hide his smile.

"Tate, that's not what I think. I live here. This is my house too, right? Don't you want me to feel at home? How can I if you won't let me pay my share? And hello, in case you haven't noticed, I'm a firefighter. It's not the kind of salary my father makes. Between the two of us, we do fine. But the whole after-my-money argument is based on what my parents have, not what I have. We can talk more about how we'll split the bills after the sex. You've avoided the conversation so far but this situation wouldn't have been as bad if we'd talked more openly about finances before."

He wet a fingertip and drew it over the hardened point of her nipple, making her arch into his touch. Pinching it enough to make her moan, he bent to kiss the hollow of her throat and across her collarbone as her free hand slid down his back.

Tate needed him so much right then she felt like she'd die from want. Needed to feel that reconnection with him, making them two as one again.

She knew he hadn't broken off with her but it hurt that he'd beg her to reveal something and then leave. Still, hearing that he'd felt like a failure, knowing she'd hurt him when she'd only meant to protect him made her realize just how important it was that they communicate with each other.

He kissed down her neck to first one nipple and then the other. She grew wetter, felt her pussy ready for him. The bristles of his beard abraded over the sensitive flesh of her breasts and what started out gentle took on an edge as they both realized the intensity of their need.

"Matt, please, please," she murmured and he kissed down her belly and settled between her thighs.

"Glad to oblige, Venus." He pulled her open with his thumbs and looked at her for long moments. It should have weirded her out, the way he gazed at such an intimate part of her body but instead, it made her feel beautiful.

Even more when his thumbs slid inside her and his mouth finally brushed across her, tongue flicking quickly over her clit until she panted. He backed away, licking slowly, avoiding her clit until she arched her hips into his face like a floozy.

He rolled her over and pulled her hips up. He'd never taken her quite like that before and it thrilled her. She pushed back against him and he laughed. "All in due time. I haven't finished what I started."

With that, he spread her thighs wide and bent, his mouth finding her again, making her groan into the pillow. With his hands on her upper thighs, he held her wide and steady as he devoured her. All she could do was hold on and be glad she walked as much as she did so her legs were strong enough to hold her up despite her trembling muscles.

Edging into her, sharp and bright, the pleasure of her climax burst over her emotions as the depth of her love for Matt Chase rushed through her.

She wasn't sure exactly what she said but whatever it was, the neighbors probably heard it, she said it so loud.

She didn't have much time to wonder though because

within moments, Matt's cock began to press into her pussy, her body parting for him, accommodating him as it always did because she was made for him.

"So beautiful. Do you have any idea how beautiful you are right now, Tate? The curve of your back, creamy and pale, your hair like moonlight against your shoulders? Spread out before me like a banquet and I didn't get nearly enough to eat."

She squeaked at the rough eroticism of his words but there was no denying he turned her on.

"You're mine, Tate. From the first moment I saw your face you worked your way into me. Mine. No one else's. Even when I'm an ass, you're mine. Even when you hide things you should tell me and your brother throws beer in my face. Even when you scrub the toilet with my toothbrush, minx. You're mine as I'm yours and we're getting married. You got me?"

Surprised but still realizing there was no way she'd say no, she nodded enthusiastically into the pillow.

"You realize I just asked you to marry me, right?"

"Yes," she managed to gasp out and he reached around and toyed with her clit, idly, as he fucked into her body.

"You're not going to argue with me?" Amusement laced his voice and she tightened herself around him, bringing a grunt from him.

"Do you want me to? What, it's just idle sex talk?" She smiled, pushing back against his thrusts.

"Seeing as how I've wanted to ask you for months, it's not idle at all. Holy...damn Tate...that was...shit!"

Laughing, she tightened again and swiveled.

"Oh it's gonna be that way, is it?" He leaned over her body and bit the flesh where shoulder met neck as his fingers on her clit sped. In that position he totally controlled everything, her movement, his depth and speed. It was beautiful and erotic. He was nearly a foot taller than she was, muscled and very strong but she knew he'd never hurt her.

And today had only underlined what she'd already come to learn—even emotional hurts would be something they could get past because, as improbable as it seemed, he was the one.

Unbelievably, another climax hit just as he pressed hard, fingers digging into her hip, the others still playing against her clit, teeth dug into her shoulder. A long groan came from him and she realized then he wasn't wearing a condom. The third time in a few weeks. Moments later she realized she never wanted him to again either.

He fell back against the bed and pulled her against him. "I love you, Tate. With everything I am. Will you marry me?"

"I love you, Matt, with everything I am. So yeah."

"You make me very happy. I'm sorry we didn't make each other happier earlier today."

"It's gonna happen. I'll try to keep my family from moving you out next time. I know my family, or my parents, are a mess. I'd understand if you were wary of that."

"Tate Murphy, I love you and your crazy brothers and sisters. My family loves you all. Your father, after Shane speaks with him and you get yourself a protection order in place, won't be an issue. My father would be happy to guide you through the process and Cassie too. She's done the protection order thing before."

"And it protected her really well."

"Hey." Reaching back, he turned on the lamp and looked at her closely. "That was a very different situation. In the first place, I know how much of a priority Petal's law enforcement puts on protection orders and family violence prevention. Shane, even before Cassie, cared and now the department is even more committed. I'm here too. And my dad is the best attorney around and the judge who hears protection orders is really good. First thing you need to do is tell him he's not getting a dime from you again. And then we'll take the next steps."

Chapter Thirteen

Christmas Day and the Chase's home was filled to the absolute rafters and Polly was in her element. Tate bustled around the kitchen along with Maggie, Matt's aunt and both his grandmothers.

The backyard held a makeshift touch football game with players from one to ninety-five. Fourteen Murphys plus Royal, Anne's boyfriend, twenty various Chases and Cassie's brother visiting from California wandered around laughing, talking, snacking and laying out plates and preparation for breakfast.

Tate had made a turkey and a ham at their house, Maggie also made a roast beef and another turkey and Liv brought a ham as well. Add to that the three turkeys and two hams Polly had baking and the side dishes nestled in Tate's, Maggie's, Liv's and Cassie's kitchens and they were good to go for dinner. But for the moment, they needed to finish up breakfast so they could get the presents as the kids were begging every three minutes.

After dishing up the scrambled eggs and putting a lid on the large bowl, Tate grabbed Lise from Liv, who laughed at Polly's snort.

"Y'all never let me hold those babies. Stingy, every last one."

Tate snickered. She'd had to race to get to Lise first because Polly hogged every baby and child in sight. Her own nieces and nephews included. She glanced at Liv over the baby's head. "I think she looks more like you every day. Her hair is so dark but she does have green eyes like her daddy."

Liv grinned. "She's so amazing. I never imagined it would be like this, you know? Marc's so good with her too. Gets up with her in the middle of the night, rocks her."

Tate nodded. "You're very fortunate to have such wonderful parents and grandparents, Lise," she crooned to Lise before kissing her forehead.

"And such wonderful aunties too." Maggie picked up Nicholas who'd run in with Kyle on his heels.

Everyone else filed in and sat at the long tables. Edward at the very head, Polly on his right. Matt put an arm around the back of Tate's chair, his nearness bringing the reality of the moment home. How fortunate was she? Despite the blight of her parentage, she had amazing brothers and sisters and a new extended family with the Chases. Her life was very good.

Edward rose. "Welcome and Merry Christmas one and all. I'm not one to talk a whole lot. Because Polly doesn't let me get a word in edgewise." Everyone laughed, including Polly. "But today I have to tell you all how truly thankful I am. My goodness look at you all. My boys grown into men. It was just yesterday wasn't it, that I had to yell at you to get your cleats off the front porch? You wanted to borrow the car for a date? You lost your first tooth?" He had to pause a moment, pressing a hand to his stomach.

"And today you're here, two of you with children of your own and finer babies I've yet to see. Polly and I have been gifted with four new ready made grandchildren in Belle, Sally, Shaye and Danny. I admit to my share of worries at first with the bird-brained women you used to squire around but you never brought anyone home who wasn't perfect. Maggie, girl I just adore you. You came into our lives and you brighten them every day. Your fire and caring, the way you mother my grandson, I'm proud to have you in this family."

Maggie gave him a wobbly smile and blew him a kiss.

"And you, Cassie. When Shane brought you here that first time I was simply bowled over by your beauty. Truly, there are few women walking this earth who are as physically stunning as you are. And yet, what sticks with me every day when I think of you is how strong you are. How much you give to Shane, how much courage and tenacity you have. You're every inch a match for my oldest."

Cassie leaned into Shane and blinked back tears.

"Livvie. Oh girl, you knocked my Marc out, you know that? I remember him coming over here and telling me about his feelings for you. Smart. Blunt. I love that. You say what you feel and you decided what you wanted and went for it. That's the kind of girl my boy needed. You're a good woman, Olivia. A beautiful mother and a fine wife and you keep Marc out of trouble. You two were made for each other. Happy first anniversary."

"Thank you, Edward. If it weren't for Marc and Polly, I'd have snapped you up already."

He winked at her and chuckled before his eyes settled on Tate.

"And Tate. Well your path here, like my other daughters, hasn't been an easy one. When I watched you stand up in court and tell the judge about your father, I realized something about you. You're small but your heart, your courage is large. Even with extortion threats, you cared about the man who'd harmed you. And you let Matt in, and you let him help and you let him love you. Each time I wondered if you'd run away from the ugliness some in this town have hurled your way, you stood up and you stuck it out.

"Matt is a good man but you don't let him coast. You appreciate the outside of my boy, but you love the inside. Polly told me about how you told her why you loved Matt earlier this year. And then you and I had lunch. I came over to your house on a Sunday and you made me a very lovely meal and we sat and talked. Your eyes, when you talked about Matt, your eyes practically glowed. No one has known my boy as well as you. Thank you, beautiful girl, for loving my son. Welcome to our family."

Tate put her hands over her face. These people were so wonderful and they were real. They meant it.

Edward came over and hugged her. "Hey, sweetness, I didn't mean to make you cry," he said softly.

She hugged him back. "Thank you for making Matt."

Polly shook her head. "Y'all are too good to be true. I'm a lucky mother-in-law."

Matt looked around the table as his father went to sit back down but before he could speak, there was a pounding on the front door.

Tim stood and put a hand out. "Tate, you sit your butt down." He craned his neck. "If you will all excuse me a moment. It's for me."

William perked up and moved to follow.

"It's my father," Beth whispered.

"Everyone, please sit." Shane stood and put his napkin down.

Matt got up. "Don't move," he admonished before he and

the rest of the men at the table got up and left.

"Oh for goodness sake!" Tate stood. "This is ridiculous."

"Tate, let them handle this," Polly spoke. "Let Matt do this. He needs to. You exorcised that demon with the protection order. Let him feel like he's protecting you. It seems silly but that's what men like to do."

"I've ruined yet another gathering with my drama."

"You sit your butt down, Tate Murphy! I will not have you making this about you. It's not. It's about your father, who is a bad man. You all deserve better. Now you let those boys kick some tail and we'll crack the windows here to hear what's happening." Polly raised an eyebrow, daring her to disobey and moved to open the windows.

Matt felt nothing but the ice of resolve to end this bullshit once and for all. The oily fucker had come to the firehouse to try and work him for money a few weeks before and he'd sent him packing.

Tim was standing on the porch, menacing Bill Murphy when Matt came out. Shane stood in the doorway, letting Matt handle things.

"I don't know what you're doing here but as Tate is inside, you're violating the protection order even being this close." Matt stood next to Tim with William on one side and Nathan on the other.

"I been hearing around town how my girl is using you for money. I figure if you want me to keep quiet about it, you need to provide incentive."

"You're aware that this kind of thing is illegal. It's called extortion, might be considered blackmail but I'd go with extortion. You'll do more jail time that way," Edward spoke lazily from his place on the porch but Matt heard the steel in it.

231

"You've been warned to remove your carcass from this property and that you're in violation of the protection order. Get your sorry ass away from here. I'm not going to let you hurt Tate ever again, you got me? This has gone on long enough with your pathetic abuse of your daughter." Matt stepped forward, pleased to see Bill step back, his bravado failing.

"Why doesn't Tate tell me herself?"

"*We're* all telling you. You've threatened my children, you've threatened my wife, you've hurt my brothers and sisters and it's not happening ever again. I beat your ass fifteen years ago, you want another helping?" Tim asked.

"You're a weak, pathetic excuse for a human being. If the only thing that makes you feel like a man is abusing a woman a foot smaller than you who's never done a damned thing to hurt you, no wonder your wife doesn't stay at home."

Tim gave him a sideways glance that held a cringe. Matt knew he pushed hard but damn it, his woman had been terrorized for most of her life by this piece of shit, he was done trying to reason with him.

Bill lunged at him but Matt was ready and his fist was cocked back to deliver a very satisfying punch to the nose. The other man howled in pain and stumbled back. "You hit me! I'm going to sue you for assault!"

"You're on my property, you've been advised to leave and you attacked him. It was self defense and there are plenty of witnesses to say so." Edward chuckled. "Now get your drunken ass off my lawn. If you so much as look at my daughter-in-law-to-be again, or any of these children you were gifted with but threw away, I'll come up with ways to sue you until the end of time."

"I don't have anything for you to take, Chase!" Bill moved back to the sidewalk.

"Certainly not pride. But it'd amuse me to mess with you for a good long time. My grandchildren are in the house, we're having Christmas breakfast. You get on out of here."

"Go on now, Bill. You're in violation of the order and if Tate wishes it, I'll arrest you right now." Shane moved his hands to his waist.

"No, I'm just fine, Shane, thank you." Tate came onto the porch and leaned into Matt, who put an arm around her. "If he leaves now. If not, arrest him." She looked at her brothers, the Chase men and finally Matt and smiled. "Thank you. Now, food is getting cold and there are some children who want to open presents, oh and me too, so let's eat."

"I love you," Matt murmured as they walked into the house after watching Bill stalk away.

"Me too. Matt?"

He stopped and looked down into her face. "Yes, Venus?"

"You're really going to get some tonight. You're very sexy when you're tough."

He laughed, leaning down to kiss her quickly. "Thank you for letting me handle that."

"Come on already!" Liv called out from the doorway and Matt sighed, dragging Tate into the dining room.

As they ate breakfast, Polly watched the children, her grandbabies as well as her newly, ready made ones, play and laugh. Children should grow up safe and knowing they were loved.

She looked at Tate who held three-year-old Shaye, kissing the top of her hair as she buttered a pancake one handed. Polly realized the sins of the parents hadn't damaged those children. They'd pulled together and held tight against all odds. Tate

Murphy was extraordinary. Polly couldn't remember the last time Matt actually got worked up enough to get into a fist fight with anyone. Even with his brothers it was more of a wrestling thing and they'd get tired and do something else.

Shane had his share of fights, even Kyle. But Matthew had been her lazy boy, nothing got him passionate enough. Until Tate. She knew she should be frowning on two fights in a few months but in truth, it made her happy to know he'd found something worth fighting for.

"I vote we leave the dishes until after presents and then the men can clean up," Polly announced to a cheer.

Everyone adjourned into the large formal living room where the tree took up most of the front windows.

Pop, Edward's father, put on his Santa hat and began to hand out presents. The process, which in the past had taken multiple hours, lengthened as more members had been added to the family and Gramps, Polly's father, stepped in and they double teamed the effort.

At the end, nearly four hours later, after several pots of coffee and snacks throughout, Matt stood, helping Tate to her feet.

"We've got a few things to tell everyone."

Polly beamed at them and Matt slid a ring on Tate's finger.

"Finally! When's the date?" Cassie asked.

"Yesterday as a matter of fact. Tate and I got married yesterday at the justice of the peace in Riverton. Obviously if we'd gotten married here at city hall, you'd have all heard about it in two minutes."

"You did not! You eloped? Why? Matthew Sebastian Chase, you should have let us plan a big wedding for you. What's Tate going to think when we threw weddings for the other girls and not for her?"

"Aren't you happy for us, Polly?" Tate asked.

Polly jumped up and hugged them both tight, followed by forty others. So many Tate was dizzy with all the love they showed her.

"We wanted to keep it simple and quiet and it was sort of a surprise. We'd planned to announce the engagement officially today and get married in March."

"But I'll be showing by then and I'm already embarrassed enough."

Polly blinked rapidly and burst into tears, hugging Tate as she hopped up and down excitedly.

"So you're happy then? You're not mad that I um, got her pregnant before I married her?" Matt laughed.

"Mad? Oh Matthew, Tate, you've both made this day even better! A new daughter-in-law, a new grandbaby, it's all fabulous. When are you due?"

Tate took a deep breath. "August thirteenth they think. I'm afraid to even announce it this early, we just found out for sure three days ago." She winked at him and he kissed her hard and fast. "An accident but not so much." She shrugged. "More like throwing caution to the wind one too many times. And this isn't something I want to go into more detail over with all these grandparents and children in the room."

"So you can't throw us a wedding but you can throw me a shower if you like." Tate hugged Polly and her sisters all hopped around squealing with delight.

"Well, you can throw a double shower." Shane stood and pulled Cassie up with him. "We're expecting in late July, right around Nicky's birthday."

Polly had to grab Edward, who laughed delightedly.

"Always have to beat me don't you?" Matt asked Shane, grinning. "We just signed a contract to have a second story built onto the house and a back sun porch put on too. We'll live in an apartment for a few months. They should be done by May."

"An apartment? No, you'll live with us!" three different people exclaimed.

Tate looked around the room. "My heart is so full. You have no idea what you all mean to me. I used to wake up in a panic when Matt and I first started dating because I was terrified it would all disappear. And then I worried my father would ruin it. But through it all, he's been there. And you've all been there. All my brothers and sisters, my new family in you all. Thank you for believing in me and for believing in me and Matt. This baby couldn't ask for more."

Cassie hugged her and they started talking about baby stuff.

Polly stood back with Edward and looked over the room. Paper everywhere, children pushing trains and trucks, dancing around with dolls. So much love and she was so lucky to see it all, to have it all in her life.

"Each year, lamb, each year things just get better. First it was just me and you in that tiny apartment on Oak, you remember? And we had our own announcement at Christmas with Shane. And each time we brought a new baby home, our lives got bigger and better. And they grew and moved out and then Kyle brought home Maggie and so on." He kissed Polly because he couldn't do anything else. Smart, small, sexy and all his, Polly Chase had been the center of his world since he clapped eyes on her when he was just nineteen years old.

"I love you something fierce, Edward Chase."

"Ditto, lamb. We're gonna be grandparents again. I can't wait to keep on getting older and better with you."

"I can't wait until everyone leaves so we can get better when we're naked."

Edward laughed, heart racing and thoughts wandering, just what she'd intended.

About the Author

To learn more about Lauren Dane, please visit www.laurendane.com. Send an email to Lauren at lauren@laurendane.com or join her messageboard to join in the fun with other readers as well.

www.laurendane.com/messageboard

Cocktail hour will never be the same.

A Man for Marley
© *2007 Arianna Hart*

Marley Sullivan is willing to do almost anything to claim her inheritance, even if it means putting up with sexy Hunter O'Malley for six months. Marley has worked hard for years turning O'Malley's Pub into a New York hot spot. This is her chance to finally own it; all she has to do is live, work, and not fall in love with Hunter.

Racecar driver Hunter O'Malley thinks being stuck working at his family's bar for six months is a fate worse than death. If he could get Marley to stop bristling at him and use her ever so kissable mouth for something other than ordering him around, it might not be so bad. But when heated tempers lead to hot lust, will six months be long enough after all?

Available now in ebook and print from Samhain Publishing.

Printed in the United States
132475LV00002B/143/P